A soft screech was my only warning before something shot out from under the dresses and began flapping around my head. We both ducked, but whatever it was grabbed hold of some of my hair and started burrowing. Tiny claws scratched my neck and scalp. "Eww, get it off, get it off!"

Nick planted his hands on my shoulders, but the thing kept tangling itself in my hair. "Be still and I'll uh...You said not to touch them."

I had a gargoyle in my hair. A baby gargoyle. Fantastic. "It's not going to pee on me, is it?"

Discord Jones

Save the Last Vamp for Me

Gayla Drummond

Katarr Kanticles Press

Katarr Kanticles Press
Texas, USA
Edited by Tonya Cannariato
Copyright © 2014 Gayla Drummond
Cover by Gayla Drummond

ISBN-13: 978-0692301401 (Katarr Kanticles Press)
ISBN-10: 0692301402

Acknowledgments

Super big thanks to you, the reader!

Also to my beta readers: Kate Smith, J.C. Montgomery, and Tonya Cannariato.

My House Hunney for his love and support.

Save the Last Vamp for Me

One

"Oh, hell no." That was my instant reaction upon entering Mr. Whitehaven's office and confirming the reason for the after-dark Thursday appointment. There was a vampire waiting.

Not just any vampire either, but Derrick. He smiled, arranging the ivory lace flowing from the cuffs of his hunter green, antique-looking jacket. He'd been changed young, so no crinkles appeared at the corners of his dark brown eyes. His hair was brown too: An incredibly disciplined mop of light brown curls that reached his shoulders. The blond streaks artfully decorating it were fake, because "vampire" equals no sunning. He looked as though he should be gracing the cover of a Gothic romance.

Mr. Whitehaven's office was the largest in our building, a nearly square space at the end of both the hallway and the building. One wall sported floor-to-ceiling shelves, fronted by glass doors. The doors were locked with a spell. I'd seen the boss open them once, to pull out a sword and dagger capable of killing demons. There was an entire treasure trove of curiosities on those shelves I'd never quite managed to find the time to delve into. Considering the massive amount of shiny, all of it was probably worth quite a lot of money.

Of course, Mr. Whitehaven was wealthy. He drove an expensive SUV, and being eight feet tall, more than likely had to have his suits custom made. I also knew he was one of the first supes to start a business after the Melding, and one of the most successful of them at that endeavor.

His long hair, always neatly smooth, was the white of new-fallen snow, and his eyes were reddish brown. I'd seen them glow crimson a couple of times in the past. He looked large, but sort of gaunt, as though he'd once had more meat on his bones. Probably as a much younger man.

While I didn't know exactly how old he was—asking some supes their ages could result in a headache from simply trying to comprehend their answers—I did know he was really, really old. Possibly ancient. Yet not a wrinkle or age spot marred his skin, even though he appeared to have a light tan.

I'd been told my boss was a highly respected member of the supe community.

Too bad that respect didn't extend to his employees like diplomatic immunity. Then again, it didn't keep the occasional elf from trying to pull a fast one either.

I didn't return the vampire's smile, too busy meeting my boss's reddish-brown gaze. "I don't work for vampires."

"No." Mr. Whitehaven agreed in his usual deep, calm baritone. "You're in my employ."

While we stared at each other, Nick slipped past me to take a seat on the couch. My boyfriend and partner wore a faint grin, because he finds the fact I always cave to our boss funny. Probably because he never wins when we argue.

I managed a whole minute before heaving a loud sigh. "Fine."

Once I'd plopped down on the couch next to Nick, Derrick chuckled. "You're still holding a grudge?"

"Your goons destroyed my car."

"I'm paying for the repairs."

"And you beat up my friend." The friend being Logan Sayer, a tiger shifter I'd met the same night the vamp and I had had our first face-to-face.

"We didn't kill him, and he wasn't exactly easy to 'beat up', Miss Jones."

I glared. "And you cracked my freaking skull."

Derrick pursed his lips, his brows drawing slightly together. "I do apologize for that. I overreacted due to your reputation of being a bit hot-headed."

I did have a tendency to roast vampires, using pyrokinesis, when they didn't back off. Under the circumstances that night, he was lucky I hadn't roasted first and asked questions later. Not really having a good comeback, I crossed my arms and kept glaring.

Childish of me, but that's how I react sometimes. I was fifteen when the Melding occurred and all the supernatural types rejoined Planet Earth. Not that I had experienced that craziness, because I passed out at exactly midnight, and spent three years in a coma. Things had mostly settled down by the time I woke up—not that I paid attention to any world-level changes then. Imagine passing out as a fifteen-year-old and waking up eighteen. Next, imagine right after being told you weren't exactly a kid anymore, you discovered you had a bushel of psychic abilities you had no clue how to control. Then toss on discovering your parents were divorced, and that your dad had remarried.

Short version, I'd been a little busy with figuring out mental and emotional things and working at physical therapy for a while. Though my twenty-third birthday was less than two weeks away, I often felt younger.

Nick patted my leg, his grin full-fledged and his chocolate brown eyes bright. He was a shifter—wolf—the boss had hired to babysit me a few months before. "Show some courtesy to the client."

I thought about sticking out my tongue at him, but didn't. He'd said the same thing I often told Percy, the parrot familiar of Kate, the final member of Arcane Solutions. He was right, because you should always be polite to those who made it possible for you to earn a living. Since I was busy house hunting, and had four new dependents, continuing to earn a living topped my list of 'Important Things to Do'.

Pasting on a smile, I looked at the vampire. "What's the case?"

"I'm here on behalf of our council, on the matter of six murders over the past month."

"Humans?" When he shook his head, I couldn't resist. "Not seeing the problem."

"I've yet to finish. It's a political issue, as all six were members of the current majority party." The vamp paused, studying me. "There are two main parties, Miss Jones. The majority party, which I'm also a member of, prefers to treat humans as donors rather than prey."

"The other party's gung-ho on the prey thing."

"Unfortunately, yes, and it's a public relations nightmare."

"I bet." Boy, did I. Something the supernaturals had quickly figured out were the strides humans had made in weapons technology. Technology in general meant humans weren't as easy to scare, or to hunt. From what I'd heard, things like ultraviolet lights had been a big shock to them, vampires in particular. And with the vamps gathered in one location, bombing them wouldn't be a problem.

"As long as we continue to hold the majority on the council, we can limit the number of human deaths. However, we are the majority party by a slim margin, and three of the victims held council seats. Those empty seats will be filled by whomever can gain enough support to take them."

"So, what exactly do you think I can do that you can't? You're a powerful telepath, and I doubt you have the same scruples I do about digging around in other people's minds."

Derrick chuckled. "That's exactly why I can't lead the investigation. I'm biased in favor of my party, therefore motivated to discover a conspiracy to weaken it."

"Maybe you don't know this, but Cordi's pretty biased too," Nick said.

"I'm fully aware of Miss Jones' prejudice against my kind. She would prefer we didn't exist, which makes her relatively impartial. I'm certain she won't hesitate to make her displeasure over being forced to work with vampires clear."

I said, "Maybe I'd dance on your ashes if every vamp in Santo Trueno spontaneously combusted, but I'm going to do my best to save human lives. So that kind of makes me less prejudiced toward those of you who don't want to kill people."

"This isn't a matter that can be handled by human police. You're a psychic, therefore not human, and thus, the only acceptable investigator to handle the matter since I'm unable to. All members of the council agreed to hiring you." He glanced at Mr. Whitehaven before adding, "Of course, due to your well-known dislike of us, being in the Barrows as often as you'll need to be will increase the likelihood of attempts on your life."

"Pfft." I waved my hand, pretending confidence I didn't really feel after that statement, and wondering if I should dispute his "not human" remark. "I've been there plenty of times without getting killed."

"Be that as it may, I suggest that you bring more than your partner." He lifted his chin, indicating Nick. "You're an ally of the White Queen. Ask her for another bodyguard or two, and consider bringing your hound as well."

"I'll take that under advisement." I was definitely doing both, the first as soon as possible.

"Excellent. If you'll come to my residence at seven tomorrow evening, I'll have everything we've gathered so far ready for you."

"Sure." I didn't need the address, since I knew exactly where he lived.

The vampire stood, inclining his head at my boss. "My thanks for your assistance."

"You're welcome."

Derrick gave me a nod next. "Miss Jones."

I nodded back, and he left the office. No one spoke until we heard the squeak of the glass door that signaled the vamp had left the building. I frowned. "This is going to be fun."

My boss ignored that in favor of changing the subject. "Have you found a new domicile yet?"

An irresistible subject change. I'd had to move home, and the overcrowding was driving me crazy. Not to mention, I worried constantly that someone of a not-friendly persuasion might follow me or otherwise find out where I was living. That would put my mom and Tonya at risk.

"Not yet, but we're going to look at another place tomorrow. Apartments are out, and there's been something wrong with all the houses I've looked at so far. Too many neighbors too close, or too small, and a lot have needed work."

Nick threw in his opinion. "She's really picky."

"Yes, I am. It needs to be as close to perfect as possible because it's a long-term investment. A house is one of the most expensive purchases people can make." I didn't want to end up with a money pit, because the idea of a mortgage was scary enough.

We chatted with the boss for a bit, before leaving to have a late dinner, something we'd been doing a lot. Work had been steady, and privacy hard to come by. After all, I was living with two other women and what felt like four dozen dogs.

"Am I staying the night?" Nick asked while we waited for our steaks. We'd picked a place that had recently opened, and I swayed a little to the rock music playing just loud enough. We'd been seated near the grill, which had been designed to be a focal point of the dining area, the rest of the kitchen tucked away behind it. Burning mesquite scented the air, and the sizzle of steaks made my mouth water.

It's always all about the steaks, so I hadn't given the place my seal of approval yet.

"Sure. Just remember to be quiet when we go in. Mom's been putting in a lot of hours, trying to set things up for the Halloween dinner for the homeless."

He promised he would be, but that promise was blown out of the water a little later, when we walked into the house and the Chihuahuas went nuts. Normal dogs didn't like shifters in general, but they really didn't like wolf shifters. My Pit Crew, as I'd taken to calling Bone, Red, and Diablo, ex-fighting dogs, tolerated him because I'd asked them to, as did Kyra, Tonya's Husky.

But the Chihuahuas refused to ignore his presence each time he walked into the house, alerting everyone that one of the "stinky animal people" had arrived. Even Speck, the youngest of them, joined in though Nick had made great efforts to become friends with him since I planned to keep the little, black pup.

I heard my mom's bedroom door open as we tried to shush the yapping. "Cordi?"

"Yeah, sorry, Mom. Nick's staying the night."

"All right. I'll see you two in the morning." Her door shut again. Tonya didn't appear or say anything, so she'd either slept through the noise, or had grown used to it enough not to worry.

"Okay, seriously, enough," I told the Chihuahuas. "Back to bed."

They grumbled and fussed, but returned to the various spots they slept in around the living room and settled down.

I grabbed Nick's hand, waved at my Pit Crew lying on the couch, and hauled him behind me to my room with Speck prancing before us.

Two

I glanced at my phone, where I had the map feature on-screen. "It's just ahead, on the left."

Nick nodded in response. He hadn't exactly been onboard with my house hunting idea at first, but after nearly a month of my living at my mom's, most of his discontent had faded. Last night had cleared the rest away, since he'd run into Tonya while returning from the bathroom. He'd been wearing my short, purple robe with little pink hearts dotted all over it.

Scrunched in the back seat of Nick's truck was most of my crew: The pit bulls and hound would be reporting back to Speck on the living situation I found for us. The five canines would all be living with me. Leglin, the hound, was bound to me by blood magic. Bone, Diablo, and Red were strays when I ran into them, and before that, each had done time in a dogfighting ring. They bore the scars to prove it.

"There's the sign. You'd have a lot of privacy out here," Nick observed. Thick evergreen bushes that were taller than he was lined each side of the two-lane road. The realtor's sign he'd mentioned was barely visible. "How many acres?"

"Twenty-four." My dog buds needed room to roam, and with other issues to consider, I'd given up on the idea of a house inside the city. One issue, the most important, was not having any close neighbors who might end up cannon fodder. On paper, this house looked to have everything my dad and I had listed as needs. It had been on the market long enough that the price had dropped several times, bringing it down enough to be affordable for me. The most major downside to it was that it'd take me a half-hour or more to drive to work every day, even though it was only a couple of miles outside city limits. "Ooh, the drive's paved. Good."

Nick turned his truck down the drive. "Lots of trees."

"Yeah." I glanced back at the dogs. "What do you guys think so far?"

"*I'm a city dog.*" Diablo, a black pit missing part of one lip, gave a disparaging sniff. Leglin nosed his shoulder before looking at me.

"*We will be happy wherever you choose, Mistress.*"

The super-sized black and tan hound's eagerness to please put a smile on my face, even though I said, "We all need to like the new place, not just me."

"I think I like it," Nick said as the house came into view. "But it needs a paint job."

"Yeah." I stared at the two-story house, taking in the peeling white paint on the window frames and porch. The siding was some sort of charcoal gray rock. "No one's lived here for nearly eight years, but Rita said everything checks out and is up to code."

None of the windows were broken. The wide front porch, which ran the length of the house, didn't look like it was sagging anywhere. The drive went to a detached two-car garage on the right side of the house, ending at the concrete pad in front of it. A sidewalk led to the front porch steps, between strips of nearly knee-high grass. "Needs mowing too. You guys watch out for snakes, okay?"

A chorus of assent sounded from the back seat as Nick parked in front of the garage and turned the truck's engine off. "Ready?"

"Yeah." I bounced out, hoping the house would prove to be the One. It was fun looking at houses, but a lot of stress too, trying to pick one that had everything we required, was within my budget, and didn't need a lot of expensive work. After all, we'd be in whichever one we selected for a long, long time. Pulling the strip of paper with the code for the key lockbox out of my purse, I said, "Inside first."

We exited the truck and trooped up to the front porch. Once I had the key in hand, I unlocked the door, and pushed it open. "Wow."

The house had undergone remodeling a few times, and currently boasted a mostly open plan on the ground floor. Standing at the door, I took in the living area to the left—with a fireplace!—that flowed into a dining area, and was set slightly apart from the kitchen by a breakfast bar. A staircase led up to the second floor. I walked in and looked into the first door on the right. "This is the den." It was a decent-sized room with built-in shelves. Moving down to the next door, I found a half-bath. "Guest bathroom." The last door led into a utility room with a door leading out to the back porch. Turning from it, I walked directly into the kitchen.

It had loads of granite countertops and cabinet space, a deep double sink with a window facing the backyard over it, and the stove and fridge were stainless steel. A few small additions, and it'd be a chef's dream. "I want this kitchen."

"Let's look upstairs." Nick grabbed my hand and pulled me across to the staircase. We thumped up them to discover the landing was a rectangle that ran the length of the house. A half-wall around the stairway made certain no one would fall while stumbling around in the middle of the night.

Windows at each end of the landing gave plenty of light. I shivered, excitement beginning to build. So far, this house seemed perfect.

Nick let go of my hand to poke his head inside the first door to the left of the stairwell. "Bedroom. How many are there?"

"Three, plus a bonus room." I joined him, slipping past to look at the room. The closet was sort of small, but I was already designating it as Leglin's room. The hound had asked to have one of his own. He wouldn't need much closet space.

A Hollywood-style bath ran between it and the other bedroom on that side. Across the landing, we walked into the master bedroom. "Okay, I love this house."

There was a pair of French doors leading out to a second story, roofed porch over the back one. The master bath had a shower stall and a corner garden tub. Nick had to drag me out to check out the linen closet set between the master bedroom and the bonus room.

"This one's really small." He stretched his arms out after walking into the bonus room, fingertips brushing the walls on either side.

"I'll use it for storage." We both noticed the string hanging from the ceiling. "Attic access."

He took hold and pulled. I helped unfold the ladder so we could go up. A pile of boxes lay in one corner of the otherwise empty space. I waited while he carefully walked across the plywood flooring, checking for weakness. "Sturdy, and I don't see any sign of termites."

"Great." I'd already decided, and hoped none of the dogs had any objections. I wanted this house. It had all the space we needed, and wouldn't need more than cleaning, new paint, and maybe carpet to make it livable.

Bone met us at the foot of the attic ladder, his one ear perked. "*I like it. Red likes it. Diablo's pulling his usual, but he likes it too.*"

"Good." That only left Leglin. I caught him on the landing. "This would be your room."

The hound went into the bedroom, sniffing around the baseboards, and then looked out the window, which faced the back of the house. He made a faint sound and headed for the other bedroom, checking the view from its window, which faced the front of the house. "*I'd prefer this one, Mistress.*"

"Sure." The secondary bedrooms were basically the same size. Leglin had also asked for a human bed, and either room was big enough for a full-size version. "Whichever one you want is fine by me. So you like the place?"

"*Yes.*" His tail wagged gently, just brushing my leg. "*I do.*"

I turned a grin on Nick, who stood in the doorway. "We're going to take it."

He smiled. "Good. The entrance to our territory is only about five miles away. I can be here in less than ten minutes."

"Cool." I threw my arms around his neck and kissed him. The nearness meant an end to one of our ongoing problems concerning my tracking ability. I could call him whenever it popped up, and he'd be here by the time I'd finished dressing.

Nick had invited me to meet his parents, but we'd had to put that on hold for the time being, between work and house hunting. I'd already met his brother, Patrick. We didn't get along well, because

Patrick was a douchebag.

"Let's go check outside."

First up, the garage. I was surprised to discover a small, unfinished efficiency apartment tucked behind the back wall. "I don't remember seeing this in the list of features."

"You could have it finished and rent it out if you needed to. Or do some kind of trade with someone who'd take care of mowing and stuff," Nick suggested.

"Maybe." I'd have to think about that, plus there'd be the expense of finishing it to consider. We left the garage and checked the other two outbuildings. One was a well house, the other just a small storage shed with a concrete floor. I didn't bother walking the entire property, because the dogs would check out everything when we had more time, but did note that there was a short post and rail fence embedded in the evergreens lining the front sections of the property.

"It's perfect. We are definitely taking it." I pulled out my cell phone to call my dad, who'd volunteered to help me navigate the scariness of first-time home ownership. "Would you lock up?"

"Sure." Nick took the house key and disappeared around the corner. I stood in the overgrown backyard, the dogs sniffing around not far away, and made what felt like a truly momentous call.

I was buying a house.

Three

After leaving what I hoped would be my future home, we took the Pit Crew home before heading for the Palisades and the tiger clan's garage. I had to wonder if the fact we caught every red light was a result of Nick's reluctance to go there. At least he let me pick the music. I sang along with Blondie while holding an imaginary mic, and ignored the amused glances of other drivers. Once there, Nick and Leglin stayed in the truck while I headed inside.

The first person I saw was Logan, and the view wasn't bad, since he was nearly waist deep in the maw of a truck, his jeans clinging in a fashion guaranteed to draw eyes. I had to reflect on how wrong it was that I could recognize him from behind like that. *Stop ogling your friend, Cordi.* "Hey."

Logan backed away from the truck and turned. "Hi. Problem with your car?"

"It's running like a top." His dark brows drew slightly together, so I added, "That's a good thing."

"Oh. Hadn't heard that one before. Did you want to see Terra?"

"Maybe? I kind of have a favor to ask, and I'm not sure which of you I should ask."

His lips quirked. "Ask me, and I'll pass you to her if necessary."

"Okay. I have a case that's going to have me in the Barrows a lot, and...."

"You need more backup."

"Yeah. I have Nick and Leglin, but I don't want to take my other three boys down there." As far as I knew, only shifters considered normal dogs threats.

"I'd be happy to help out, but I really need to stay close to Terra."

"I know that, no problem."

He glanced around at the other men, who were all busy working on various cars. "Soames has been with me the longest. He's a good fighter, alert, and follows orders."

"Anyone you trust is cool."

"I trust him with Terra's life." From Logan, that was probably the highest compliment he could pay someone.

"You won't be short-handed, will you?" Nothing had been settled concerning the other tiger shifters, led by a large, overly muscular man I liked to call the Mega-Douche. He wanted Terra as his Queen, an idea that didn't exactly thrill the seventeen-year-old. They'd made another attempt to kidnap her three weeks before, but Logan and the rest of the clan had stopped them.

He smiled. "No, we've had a few more people join us. I can spare Soames for a while."

"How many is a few?" Geeze, how long had it been since I'd last talked to them? Two weeks? Yes, that long. I'd had lunch with Terra and Logan, other members of their clan spread around the restaurant and keeping watch for trouble.

"Five more, and one's an older queen with the same talent Alanna has for crowd control. Two of the men are related to her. We're lucky to have them."

"Good. I just realized what a terrible ally and friend I've been lately. I've only seen you guys twice since the Case of the Cursing Corpsicle."

Logan chuckled. "It's okay. You've been busy, and we've mostly been staying close to home. Safer for Terra that way, even though she's about to climb the walls."

I felt awful, hearing that. "Sunday, my mom's planning to put together some care packages for the homeless. Tonya and I are going to help her, but we could use another person or two. I could teleport you two over and back home afterward, so no one would know. Oh, and there will lunch, cookies, and dinner."

"Cookies are hard to turn down. I'll let Terra know, but it's probably safe to accept."

"Cool. It'll be fun, and it's for a good cause too."

"Right." He raised his voice a bit. "Soames."

Soames slid out from under a car. "Yes?"

"Go clean up. You'll be working with Discord for a couple of weeks."

I hoped it didn't take that long, watching Soames sit up before rising to his feet, a grin appearing on his face. "Bodyguard, or do I get to be an honorary PI?"

"How about both?" I suggested, having learned that shifters could be quite the Noticers of Things.

"Great. Sounds fun. I think I have oil in my hair, so give me twenty to shower and change."

"That'll work, thanks."

He nodded and jogged to the door that lead to the stairwell of the attached apartment building. I looked at Logan. "Has he crossed paths with vampires before?"

"A few times. Between the four of you, I doubt you'll have too much trouble down there."

I liked that Logan never failed to count me as a fighter, instead of labeling me as cannon fodder, or the next best thing to it. "Tell me something: Did you charge for labor when you rebuilt my car?"

"Didn't plan to," he admitted, his pine green eyes scanning the garage before meeting mine again. "Not until you told me the vamp was paying the bill. Him, I charged double."

"Should've charged triple." We shared a laugh.

"Let me guess, he's your client."

I raised both eyebrows. "You're getting better and better at this detective stuff."

Logan winked. "One day, I'll open my own agency and give you a run for your money."

"You do that. A little healthy competition's good for the soul."

We chatted until Soames returned. "I'm ready."

"I'll make sure he gets home. We're in Nick's truck because of Leglin. I may have to get a second vehicle, with all these dogs to cart around."

"You can use one of our trucks whenever you need to," Logan said. "Just let me know."

"That's nice of you. Thanks, I'll do that. Tell Terra I said 'hi', okay?"

"Will do. See you later, Discord."

"Bye." Soames and I left for Nick's truck. I climbed in the front seat first, and made introductions while the tiger shifter followed me. Leglin had the whole back seat to himself. "We're going to grab dinner first. Our meeting's not until seven."

"Sure." Soames pulled on his seat belt. "How much do I need to know?"

"Vamps don't tend to feel friendly toward me."

He laughed. "Knew that. Saw your car."

"Right. Okay, we've been hired by Lord Derrick to investigate some murders that appear to be politically motivated."

He nodded, using his forefinger to whisk a few hairs out of his eyes. "So I watch your backs and keep my eyes open for anything useful."

I nodded. "Pretty much. Leglin's going to be watching all of our backs."

"Okay, can do." He leaned forward to look past me at Nick. "Nice truck."

"Thanks."

"What kind of gas mileage does it get?"

I managed to keep from sighing as they began talking trucks. At least they were getting along, without any sniping from Nick. That was kind of interesting, since he'd taken an intense dislike to Logan practically on sight, and had tried to talk me out of having anything to do with Terra. He was convinced Logan was interested in me, even though Logan had never flirted or anything.

Logan was friendly, but no more so than either Damian or David, two of my witch buddies. Maybe Nick wasn't being his usual jealous self because I'd already stepped into the shifter political arena by helping Logan run the Douche and his followers off a couple of times? Like a spilled milk kind of thing?

Of course, my boyfriend had spent a few days trying to convince me to renounce being their ally, but he'd finally given up when I told him I wouldn't go back on my word. We hadn't discussed it since.

Which was fine by me, because we argued about plenty of other things. For someone who'd said he loved me and had been prepared to propose, Nick had a lot of trouble accepting me for who I was.

That didn't exactly bode well for a future together, but I was willing to let things go for a while. He was the first boyfriend I'd had who took extra time in the bedroom to make certain I had as much fun as he did, and without my having to explain or ask.

He was a good kisser, and near expert-level cuddler. Plus, he was hot.

Wow. I had a bit of a shallowness problem going on. Definitely something I should work on. It wasn't as though Nick didn't have other, more important qualities. He was faithful, had a good sense of humor, and had proven more than willing to put himself between me and physical danger. He was open to trying new things, and he really seemed to like spending time with my family, little brothers and all. A pretty good guy and person.

Whether he was the right guy for me long term, well...I'd reserve judgment.

"Earth to Cordi."

I blinked, realizing we were pulling into the parking lot of my favorite Italian restaurant. "What?"

"We're here. What are you thinking so hard about?" Nick guided his truck into a parking space.

"Girl stuff." Thinking about your boyfriend totally qualified. "Sorry, truck talk zones me out."

Inside, we placed our orders, and I looked at Soames after our server brought our drinks and left. "Logan said you'd been with him the longest."

"First chosen for Terra's clan. I was six."

I knew Logan was twenty-nine, and had been appointed Terra's Protector at age twelve. That meant Soames was twenty-three. "Soames is your last name, right?"

"Yes. According to my mother when she's mad, my name is Dane Alexander Soames."

I laughed. "My mom does that too, even to my dad. Makes us both cringe because we know we're in for it when she hauls out all three names."

"Exactly." He looked at Nick. "Does your mother do that too?"

"To Patrick a lot, but not so much to me. I don't make her mad very often."

"It doesn't surprise me that you're the good son, and he's the hell raiser," I said. "Not even a little bit."

Nick scrunched his face. "He's not a warl...oh, that's one of those weird human sayings." He pursed his lips. "Yep, he's the hell raiser. It's really annoying."

"He's really annoying." I changed the subject, because Patrick wasn't a favorite one. Nick's older brother had a thing for hitting on his little brother's girlfriends. Patrick had told me so himself, right after hitting on me, the douchebag. "I'm hoping this case doesn't take long."

"Don't hurry on my account," Soames said. "I'll enjoy the break from being a mechanic."

"You don't like the work?"

"I like cars and trucks, but no, not working on them. You wouldn't believe how much time Logan had to spend teaching me stuff so that I could get licensed."

I suddenly wondered how Logan had learned it all, and asked. Soames grinned. "He made a deal with a brownie clan after getting his first car magazine from them."

"What?"

"Maybe we couldn't pass between the realms, but some of the smaller folk could, and that's how they survived, by smuggling stuff. Not just magazines, but all sorts of stuff."

Hm. "Stuff like, say, socks?"

"Those, toys, you name it. If they could carry it, they did."

Hah, I'd just solved one of the greatest mysteries of humankind: Why socks always went missing from dryers. "They still work the smuggling gig?"

"Sure. They're pretty small, and that kind of makes it hard for them to find jobs. They have to survive too."

"Of course," I agreed. "But how did they get here and into people's houses?"

"Magic."

"But there wasn't any here before the Melding."

Nick snorted. "There was, but it was too weak for most to use. Just not too weak for the little folk to survive on and use."

Huh, always something new to learn. I remembered something Terra had mentioned to me. "Is there a dragon living in Santo Trueno?"

The two men exchanged a look, their expressions smoothing to identical blandness. I looked from Nick to Soames, wondering why neither had answered yet. "That's a yes, right?"

They kept gazing at each other, setting my curiosity on fire, and finally, after nearly a full minute of silence, I saw Soames shrug. Nick was the one who answered. "Yes, but he's secretive, doesn't like people knowing about him."

"Why would he care?"

"I should've said 'humans', and he cares because he's a freaking dragon, Cordi. One of the few left, and one of the most powerful supes in existence."

Soames nodded. "You don't want to know what he'd do if threatened, or if people started hunting for his treasure."

"Okay." I dropped the subject even though the confirmation we had one, and it had treasure, only further fueled my curiosity. Maybe my witch buddies could tell me more. I made a note to ask them later. "Ooh, here comes our food."

Conversation during the meal consisted of my describing the house we'd looked at to Soames. "It has loads of space. I hope I'm able to get it."

"It sounds really nice. We're looking for a new place too." He wrinkled his nose. "The Palisades are too noisy, but where we're at was the best we could do at first."

"I can put you guys in touch with my realtor," I offered. "She's a family friend too. Her name's Rita."

"I'll pass that on to Logan when I get home tonight. Thanks."

"No problem." We finished a few minutes later, and left, ready to begin the night's work.

Four

"I'm never coming down here without you again," I said, my hand across Leglin's shoulders as he walked beside me. Nick was on my other side, with Soames beside Leglin. Vampires had been clearing out of the way since we'd entered the Barrows. One look at the hound, and they found elsewhere to be.

"You shouldn't go anywhere without him or me." Nick caught my hand, lifted it to kiss the back with a smug grin. "I keep telling you that."

I limited my response to an eye roll. We'd spent way too much time arguing over that since we'd met. There had been some clarification that he didn't think I was totally helpless, but even with my psychic abilities, my boyfriend thought I was a little too "fragile" to face off with supes.

He'd been on me about carrying the gun I kept in my desk drawer at the office. Mr. Whitehaven supplied everyone with guns and had paid for our concealed carry classes and licenses. Though I'd turned out to be a fair shot, I didn't like guns. When you pulled one out, you had to be ready to kill someone. I preferred knocking them unconscious if at all possible. Still violent, sure, but a lot less final than death.

Exception: Vampires. I'm fine with putting them out of everyone's misery. They're just walking, talking corpses. Predators that see people as prey. Parasites who feed on the blood of the living.

Yes, I'm prejudiced against them.

It took about twenty minutes to reach Derrick's estate. The two goons on guard at the gate didn't want to let Leglin in. I crossed my arms. "If he's not going in, neither are we. Better call your boss."

"That won't be necessary, Miss Jones."

I started, not having heard a third vampire arriving. And nearly peed myself when I turned to check him out, because he was every bit as big as the douchebag who wanted to kidnap Terra, with short, dark brown hair and dark brown eyes. Hoping no one heard my gulp, I asked, "And you are?"

"Stone. I'll be your guard while you're assisting my master." He half-smiled. "Open the gate. I'll escort Miss Jones and her companions inside."

"With my hound."

Stone inclined his head. "Of course."

The other two didn't argue, opening the gates to allow us through. Stone offered me his arm, but I pretended not to notice. I don't like touching vampires because their memories can be overwhelming and are usually bloody with a side of sex. The kinds of sex I wasn't interested in and didn't want in my head.

He changed the offer of his arm to a gesture to follow him after a second or two. We did, though Nick took hold of my free hand while I slipped the fingers of my other through Leglin's collar. I shot Soames a look, and he proved himself quick on the uptake by hooking one of his fingers through the hound's collar on the other side.

With all of us in contact, either Leglin or I could pop us all out of there in a blink.

It wasn't as though I doubted Mr. Whitehaven's judgment, but I'd rather be safe than sorry if the case turned out to be some elaborate hoax to get me into the Barrows. I had vampire enemies, and didn't trust Lord Derrick any further than I could throw him without my telekinesis. Kate had tried to research the vampire, and had come up empty, so we didn't know much about him.

Plus, Stone could break me in half, and as much as I protested being thought helpless, physically I was the weakest in our foursome. The guys and Leglin might be able to move as fast as vampires, but I wasn't going to count on that.

The vampire led us down a path of stone, bordered on each side by a hedge. Over the hedges, I could see gardens spreading out. I looked up at the eternally moonlit sky and the few streaky clouds. "How does anything grow down here without sun?"

"Magic, Miss Jones."

Of course. The Barrows was a pocket realm, and by then, I should've been used to the fact pocket realms had their own skies and weather, not to mention rules. It was kind of hard to comprehend though, because I also knew we were in a cavern, and that there were smaller caverns and tunnels beyond it, running all over, under the city.

I stopped thinking about it, because the end result was always a headache. It's magic. Best to leave it at that.

Instead, I focused on the castle ahead, a two-story pile of gray stone with a nearly windowless tower rising from the center. Though I'd never been inside, I could guess at the layout thanks to trips inside a few other castles. At least two levels of cellars; even in the Barrows, vampires seemed to prefer sleeping underground. The first would be more of dungeon than storage or sleeping space. The deeper level would house Derrick's minions during their required six hours of deady-bye.

Two more vampires, dressed in blue satin coats, short pants, and white shirts loaded with lace, stood at the ten-foot-tall double front door. They bowed as we climbed the steps, and opened the doors.

Once through, it felt as though we'd stepped a few centuries back in time. We were in the main hall, facing a wide staircase that led up to a landing, with sets of stairs on the left and right going up to the second floor. Vampires love their high ceilings, or more likely, they can't resist spying on new arrivals through the railings. I definitely felt eyes on us from above.

"This way, please." Stone led us to the left of the stairs, and past them. There was a matching set of stairs on the other side. He stopped in front of a set of heavy-looking wooden doors about halfway down the hall. "My master will meet with you in here."

"In here" proved to be a library. We filed inside and the vampire shut the doors, leaving us to look around. Two couches, upholstered in red velvet, faced each other across a low round table in the center of the room. A window directly across from the doors gave evidence of how thick the stone walls were, since there was plenty of room to climb up and lounge while reading. Which someone regularly did, judging by the number of decorative pillows and throws scattered on the ledge.

A fireplace big enough for me to walk into sat centered on the right wall. Other than it and the window, you wouldn't have known there were stone walls because the rest were covered by floor-to-ceiling shelves built from dark wood. A chandelier hung from the ceiling, directly over the round table.

I traded looks with Nick and Soames, and we split up to look at the books on the shelves. Leglin, after a glance from me, followed Soames. My first scan of the shelves at eye level put a smile on my face. "Someone sure loves reading vampire romances."

"Research," Nick said.

"What?"

"They read them to find out how humans think they'll behave, and by behaving that way, they become better hunters."

"That's cheating." Or so I felt. "Do shifters read paranormal romances too, to learn how to pick up humans?"

The guys answered a little too quickly. "No."

"Uh-huh." I squatted to take a look at the contents of the lower shelves. "You do too."

"No, we don't." Nick bent to look at a lower shelf.

"Do too."

"Don't."

I laughed, convinced he had, but refrained from throwing another "Do too" at him.

Ten minutes after Stone shut the library doors, he opened them and stepped aside to bow Lord Derrick into the room. When Derrick followed his minion into the library, the vampire lord looked like a skinny kid in comparison to Stone's muscular bulk. I wondered if the big vamp had been eavesdropping.

Derrick carried a sheaf of manila folders in one hand, and something long and wrapped in a dark blue towel in his other. Nick stepped in front of me. "What's that?"

"One of the murder weapons. I thought Miss Jones might find it useful." The master vamp laid the wrapped bundle on the table. "If you'll join me in sitting, I'll review the information we've gathered."

I ended up facing Derrick across the table, flanked by Nick and Soames. Leglin sat at the end of our couch, while Stone stood behind the other, at his master's left shoulder. We each took a folder—Derrick had four—and I opened mine immediately. Inside were sheets of paper with small photos paper-clipped to the corners.

The papers had short biographies, date and manner of death for each murdered vamp, as well as a list of their known associates. I paused on the third one, though two others looked vaguely familiar to me. The third one, I knew. "This one didn't have a problem killing people."

Derrick said, "There's a difference between killing prey and turning a willing volunteer."

"That's not what I meant."

"It's unsurprising you would have a strong dislike toward Lord Merriven after such tragic circumstances. Yet I can assure you that he was a firm proponent of treating humans as donors."

I realized I was smiling down at the photo, and stopped. The vampire was the same one who'd turned Ginger and then treated her like something he couldn't scrape off his shoe. Regardless of what people thought, I didn't go around staking or burning vampires at whim. If I did, he'd have been truly dead long before now. Regardless of Derrick's assurance, Ginger had told me otherwise in regard to her master, and in lurid detail. But I let it drop because vampires are arrogant, stubborn creatures, and because the killer, or killers, had chopped off his head. He'd been old enough to turn to dust. "Did anyone take photos of the scenes?"

"Yes. Stone, would you check on the printing progress?"

"Of course." The big vamp left the room. I looked through the rest of the file, checking each victim's manner of death and resulting remains. Three others had been old enough to turn to ash, but the last two hadn't.

The corpses of both bore the description of "fresh" which meant they'd been new vampires. "Do you know when Lira and Dalton were turned?"

"Within the past three months, judging by their final states."

I looked up again, meeting Derrick's gaze. "They weren't power players, not being that new."

"Both were turned by Lady Esme. They were reportedly favorites of hers."

I glanced at the folder again. She was the first victim. "The only reason I can think of to kill them would be if they knew who killed her. But they weren't killed at the same time. Lira was a week later, and Dalton was the last one, five days ago."

"That was my thought as well, Miss Jones."

Stone returned, handing over a thick stack of photos to Derrick, who immediately began separating them into two piles. I closed my folder to watch. Nick and Soames continued looking through their copies. "What psychic abilities do you have?"

"Telepathy is the most common among my people."

Leaning back, I crossed my arms. "That's not what I asked."

"No, it wasn't," Derrick agreed with a faint smile. "I have two others."

I pushed. "And they are?"

"I wouldn't be where I am today if everyone was aware of what my abilities are, Miss Jones. A lesson you should take to heart, especially if you're still collecting them yourself." Derrick finished sorting the photos, straightened both stacks, and slid one across the table. "Those are your copies."

I glanced at the towel-wrapped bundle and decided to try a slightly different question. "Do any vampires you know of have psychometry?"

It was the ability to handle objects and pick up, for the lack of a better word, memories from them. The theory was that the energy of something was affected by the energy of whatever else it came into contact with, leaving behind impressions. I often saw images, heard sounds, and less often, could smell or taste things. Some of those impressions didn't stay long, while others were permanently embedded. Often the less savory ones.

Unfortunately, it didn't always work the first time, and when it did, the results were often a confusing mess that took time to sort itself out into anything useful. Less often, psychometry would result in clear, vivid visions.

He answered, and threw me a bone while doing so. "None that I'm aware of, and that includes me."

I could mark off one ability for him, if he wasn't lying. I knew he was scary powerful with telepathy, and his refusal to say what his other two abilities were tickled my curiosity something fierce. Maybe I'd find out before we solved the case. "Will we have access to the scenes?"

"Of course. Stone will show them all to you, whenever you're ready."

"Thanks." I tucked the photos into my folder. "You know, we researched you back when Zoe was missing and your goons came after me the first time. Didn't dig anything up. Where do you stand in the hierarchy?"

The vampire lord smiled. "I'm merely an inquisitive cog in the machine."

"You're the Council's personal investigator."

"That is a role I play at times, yes."

I glared. "You're frustrating."

Derrick's smile widened. "I've been told that. Would you care to handle the weapon now?"

No, I wouldn't, but it was part of the job. "Sure."

Nick took my folder while Derrick slid the wrapped weapon in front of me and flipped the towel away to reveal a sword. I studied it for a minute. Greasy ashes clung to its double-edged blade. The grip was leather-wrapped, and there was a carnelian set in the pommel. The guard was straight with typical, rounded ends.

After my first few attempts to describe swords using phrases like "long pointy parts" and "part above the handle", Mr. Whitehaven had taught me the correct names for each element as well as some of the different types of swords. This one was sometimes called a short bastard sword. I glanced at Derrick. "This was used on him, right?"

He didn't ask which "him" I meant. "Yes. It was left at the scene of his death."

Interesting. Why leave the murder weapon behind? Even if the killer knew that no vampires had psychometry, there were spells that could recreate scenes of an item's last usage. Unless he or she had spelled the sword against them, if that were possible. I'd have to ask my witch buddies about that.

Leather was something that tended to absorb "memories" best. "Do you know how old this sword is?"

"It was made in the fifteenth century, though I haven't been able to determine an exact date."

Great, it was somewhere between five and six hundred years old. I sighed. "I may have to take it with me."

"Why?"

"Because the older the object, the more history it has, and some of the old things like to show me all of their history." I frowned at the sword. "In chronological order."

Lord Derrick's eyes widened as he sat back. "I've never heard that about psychometry. Only that the most recent events might be retained."

I wondered what "recent" meant to a vampire. "I don't know if that's true for everyone or not, but that's how it sometimes works for me."

"Fascinating." He looked at the sword. "The grip's wrapping is likely the newest item."

I already knew that, because that was the most likely to wear out part. The carnelian would be second, because jewels could loosen, fall out, and be lost or replaced at the whim of each new owner. It still depended on how long each had been part of the whole though. Instead of responding, I put my hand above the grip and closed my eyes before touching it.

Nothing.

I gave it a few seconds before opening my eyes to change positions, and put two fingers on the carnelian. Nothing again. Crap. Taking a deep breath, I moved my hand over the ashy blade. I really didn't want to touch the ashes while trying to use this ability, but they more or less ran the entire length of the blade. If they'd been caused by fire, it wouldn't be a problem, but he hadn't burned to death.

"Is there a problem?"

I looked up at Derrick. Yeah, there was a problem. I didn't want to learn anything more about Ginger's former master than I already had. What I knew was awful enough. "Just hoping I don't cut myself."

He smiled. "We've already fed."

"Sharing isn't caring." I closed my eyes and put my hand down. Cool metal and vampire grit. Ugh. When they didn't burn, their ashes felt like sand, the larger, heavier sort used to cover playgrounds.

My stomach flip-flopped at the sensation of flying through the air then roiled as the sword struck flesh, slicing through it with a muted growl. Or maybe the sound came from the guy using it. The sword's impression of its wielder was definitely male.

No images, just sensations. Opening my eyes and pulling my hand away, I wiped it on the towel. "Not much, other than the person who used it was a man. Do you have any hand sanitizer?"

The vampire flicked his fingers, and Stone left the room again. "If you handle it more, is there a chance you'll learn something else?"

"Yeah."

"Then feel free to take it with you, Miss Jones."

Whoopie. "Thank you."

Derrick cocked his head. "You're being quite courteous for someone who intensely dislikes my kind."

"You're a client. I'm being professional." I covered up the sword as Stone returned. The big vamp handed me a small bottle of hand sanitizer. "Thank you."

After squirting a healthy amount in one hand, I rubbed my hands together while thinking. We could start checking the scenes. I might have a retro-cognition vision, or see something useful via psychometry. My tracking ability might kick in. It would be nice if it did, and led us right to the killer or killers.

That had actually only happened once though, and in this case, if there were more than one killer, anything I picked up from each scene might end up confusing things more. "I think we'll look at the first scene tonight, work each murder through if possible, before moving to the next."

"Methodical," Derrick said. "Not something I've heard often in regard to your work habits. I believe 'fly by the seat of her pants' is the most common opinion."

"I do whatever works." As a psychic, following the PI rulebook usually went out the window. I nodded at the sword. "Can that be bagged?"

"Certainly, and Stone will escort you to Lady Esme's home." He stood, a faint curve appearing on his lips. "He'll keep me informed of your progress unless you require a meeting with me."

"Fine." The less time in face to faces with him, the better. "Thanks for the info."

"You're welcome, Miss Jones. Gentlemen." With a nod, Lord Derrick vacated the library.

Five

Lady Esme had been a petite, blue-eyed blonde turned when she was sixteen. Arriving at her "home" I thought she may have been overcompensating for her attractive appearance. It wasn't a castle with turrets, but what looked like a fort of some sort with a lot of really ugly gargoyles lining its stone walls, as well as the outer wall. Gargoyles littered the gardens, and two that somewhat resembled lions stood guard at the huge front doors.

"Spooky."

"*They live, mistress,*" Leglin said, and I shivered, edging away from the one to the left of the door that I'd been looking at. We were waiting for someone to answer Stone's knock.

"They're real? That's just creepy."

"Lady Esme had a talent for taming gargoyles." Stone smiled, and I noticed his fangs didn't show. "One of the reasons her family is few in number. She didn't need to turn many, with such a large number of gargoyles under her command."

Vamps called their groups families? I turned, craning my neck to look up and around. "How many are there?"

"Possibly as many as two hundred. There are more inside."

"So she had all these gargoyle guards, and someone still managed to kill her in her own home." That seemed to point to magic, but all the suspects were vampires and it was generally accepted that vampires couldn't do magic. Either some could, or the killer had the ability to teleport. That was the best psychic ability for getting in and out anywhere fast. "Hm."

"It's dark. They should be awake," Soames said. "Why aren't they?"

"Perhaps they're mourning the death of their mistress." Stone grasped the metal ring of the knocker and banged it a few more times. I glanced back at the open gate. There hadn't been any vamps on guard.

"Derrick said she'd turned Lira and Dawson about three months ago. Was she replacing, or growing her family?" I scratched Leglin's neck, trying to decide if it was the gargoyles or something else causing my uneasiness.

"As I said, she kept her family quite small. With those two, she had five fledglings."

Growing then, and there should be three vampires inside. I closed my eyes and scanned with my telepathy, picking up nothing but a low, grinding hum. "I don't think anyone's home."

The big vampire glanced at me before shoving one of the doors open. A pile of ashes lay ten feet beyond it, ruining the dark green carpet runner lining the main hall. He took two steps toward the ashes before I said, "Wait. Let me take pictures first."

"Of course. I'll inform my master of our discovery while you do so."

We both pulled out our cell phones, and I tapped the camera icon to turn it on. First, I took still shots, beginning with the view of the grand hall from the doorway. Once I'd finished taking all the shots I wanted, I took a few minutes of video for good measure.

By the time I'd finished, Lord Derrick himself arrived, with a passel of vampires behind him. I hurried toward the door before he stepped inside. "You hired us to do the investigating."

"Of course, but we can locate the others more quickly if they're here."

"Yeah, and mess with the evidence if it doesn't support the 'politically motivated' theory."

He glared, squaring his shoulders. "Excuse me?"

"This," I waved a hand toward the ashes. "Might be something else entirely, and I don't feel like going off on a wild goose chase if it's not related to the case you hired us to handle."

"Are you suggesting...."

"I'm not suggesting anything. Let us do our job, and once we're finished scoping things out, you and your people can do yours." I jerked my chin toward Stone. "He can go with us. I'm done with this scene, so your people can do their thing here."

We had a stare off, but Derrick finally agreed.

The guys, Leglin, Stone, and I walked past the ash pile to the foot of the stairs. There were two gargoyles perched on the newel caps, not twenty feet away from the pile of ashes. They looked like misshapen dogs with wings and smushed Pekinese faces. "Those two just stood there and watched?"

"Gargoyles are stone during the day." Soames sniffed the air. "They're supposed to come alive at nightfall."

"Okay. But can they see during the day, or are they completely unconscious?" Neither he nor Stone knew. I pulled out my cell phone and called my boss.

"Arcane Solutions, how may I help you?"

"Hi, it's me. What can you tell me about gargoyles? Specifically, do they know what's going on while they're stone?"

Mr. Whitehaven said, "The young have less patience with being constrained by daylight. They often do not sleep as deeply as their elders do."

"Okay." Maybe there was a gargoyle kid or teen I could talk to. If they were able to talk. "Any tips on figuring out which are young and how to talk to them?"

"The smaller the gargoyle, the younger it is. I wouldn't recommend attempting telepathic contact with an elder, Discordia, unless one approaches you."

"They're all still rocks."

"Interesting." He was quiet for a moment. "Look for one near the size of your smaller four-legged houseguests, and speak to it out loud so that the others will realize you have no intentions of harming it before you attempt telepathic communication. Don't touch it unless it invites you to. Gargoyles can be quite protective of their young."

"Right. Thanks, boss." I ended the call and put my phone away. "Mr. Whitehaven said not to touch the gargoyles, and I need to find a Chihuahua-sized one to try and talk to. Upstairs or down first?"

"The safest rooms would be downstairs, and if they were aware they were under attack, they should've gone to them," Stone replied.

"Then down we go."

"This way." He led us down the grand hall to an archway. Inside was an open wooden door, and a table holding oil lamps. The big vamp lit two, offering one to Soames. Beyond the wooden door were stone steps leading down into darkness.

"I thought vampires could see in the dark."

"Some habits are difficult to break," Stone said as he started down the steps. Nick scuttled a step ahead, to put himself between the vamp and me. I rolled my eyes before following him, Leglin beside me, and Soames brought up the rear, holding his oil lamp high. At the foot of the steps, we found a second pile of vampire remains.

"Great. Let me through, I need to get pictures." It took a minute to slide past the two in front. After snapping one shot, I checked the result. "Soames, will you pass that lamp to Nick? I need more light."

"Turn the flash on," Nick said.

"It's on, but the picture sucks. More light."

He took the lamp from Soames and held it out. I took as many shots as I could, and noticed a faint glint of something in the pile when shooting from one angle. "Found something. Hang on."

After digging a pen out of my purse, I crouched down and used it to fish out a gold signet ring. Holding it up for Stone to look at, I asked, "Know who this belongs to?"

"Ramon. He was Esme's heir apparent to her council seat."

"Okay. Did anyone grab...." Stone whipped out a plastic baggie from his pocket and opened it. I let the ring drop into it. "Thanks.

Keep it for now."

The men and Leglin edged around the late Ramon, and Stone retook the lead. We followed him down a low-ceilinged stone hallway, turning right to take a second flight of stairs down. "Esme's chambers are at the end of this passage."

One of Esme's family had met his or her end in the same room, and hadn't been old enough to turn to dust. A brownish skeleton lay sprawled through the doorway, its skull detached. I looked at what I could see of the room. The skull, not a foot away from the large bed dominating the chamber, was facing the door as if it had watched its body turn to bone. A pair of emerald and diamond earrings lay to either side of the skull, signaling the vamp leftovers were female. "Ugh."

"Gia," Stone murmured. "You should've listened to me."

"What did you tell her?"

The big vamp glanced at me. "That she should request sanctuary with my master."

"Oh. And you think he's safe with all of this going on?" I peered into the room. "Are you sure it's her?"

"I gave her those earrings."

"Oh. Um, my sympathies." Sympathy wasn't what I felt. Irritation over more complications in the case? Oh, yeah, I was totally feeling that. "Why would she run in here? It's a dead end."

Nearly the instant I finished speaking, a flash illuminated my mind and a pale gray thread appeared, leading into the room. I groaned and felt Nick touch my back. "What's wrong?"

"Another new color."

"Excuse me?" Stone said.

"Psychic thing. Can we get some light in there?" The light from the hallway fell in a rectangle from door to bed. The rest of the room was dark, thanks to the lack of windows.

"Of course." The big vamp stepped over his late girlfriend and began lighting candles. I followed, Nick behind me, but not before handing Soames my phone and indicating the skeleton with a jerk of my chin. He began taking pictures, and I tried not to make a face when I realized they'd left Lady Esme's ashes on her bed. The gray line led around the bed and to the far corner of the room, where a wardrobe sat against the wall.

"Maybe it's a door to Narnia," I muttered, and Nick gave me a blank look. "You only read paranormal romances, right?"

"No."

I was beginning to suspect he didn't read at all, or at least not for fun. The wardrobe's doors were cracked open. Waving Nick back, I used my telekinesis to open them all the way. It was full of evening dresses and shoeboxes. "Lady Esme, fashionista."

Nick surveyed the contents with narrowed eyes. "I don't see anything useful."

"Well, it's still showing, so something in there is a clue or leads to a clue." I stepped forward and began looking through the dresses. "Ooh, this one's nice. Wonder where she bought it?"

A soft screech was my only warning before something shot out from under the dresses and began flapping around my head. We both ducked, but whatever it was grabbed hold of some of my hair and started burrowing. Tiny claws scratched my neck and scalp. "Eww, get it off, get it off!"

Nick planted his hands on my shoulders, but the thing kept tangling itself in my hair. "Be still and I'll uh...You said not to touch them."

I had a gargoyle in my hair. A baby gargoyle. Fantastic. "It's not going to pee on me, is it?"

"Like I'd know. Quit moving." He released my shoulders and parted my hair to look at it. "It's hiding its face. I think it's scared."

"Great." He let my hair fall and I slowly turned around. "How do I get it to let go?"

"Talk to it?"

The boss had said to do that before trying telepathy. "Right. Um, little gargoyle, it's okay. You don't have to be scared. No one here's going to hurt you."

No movement from the lump attached to the back of my head. "Come on, baby G. Get out of my hair." Nothing. I looked around the end of the bed at Stone. "A little help here?"

"Perhaps if you took it upstairs to one of the larger gargoyles?"

"Okay." I glanced at the wardrobe, and noticed the gray tracking line had disappeared. Which had to mean it had appeared to point me at the baby gargoyle, and thus, the critter tangled in my hair could offer up a clue. "Yeah, I'll do that. Come on, Nick."

We rejoined Soames and Leglin after stepping over the late Gia. Stone didn't follow us, probably wanting a few minutes alone to either mourn or reclaim those expensive earrings. I waited until we cleared the stairs leading up to the main floor before trying to talk to the little gargoyle again, using my telepathy this time. *Hi, my name's Cordi. What's yours?*

It shivered.

It's really all right. I won't let anyone hurt you.

The gargoyle moved, pulling my hair. I gritted my teeth to keep from saying "Ow" and maybe scaring it more. *Do you want your mommy? If you do, you'll have to tell me where she is.*

Its tiny claws scratched as it slipped down, moving from my hair to my shoulder. Soames noticed and started to say something, but closed his mouth when I put my finger to my lips. The gargoyle huddled against the side of my neck, pulling my hair over itself to hide. It felt like warm suede. *That's more comfy. Thank you.*

Welcome. It was the tiniest whisper of thought, but clear. Yay, I'd established contact with the alien life form. Thank goodness it wasn't a face hugger.

What's your name?

Tase. It shivered again, something sliding around the back of my neck.

Though I hadn't meant to, I was already touching it—well, it was touching me—so I reached up to pat it. *Did we scare you? We didn't mean to.*

Invisible, invisible, invisible. Tase shivered while chanting the words as though they were a spell. I dropped my hand, worried I'd freaked him out by touching him.

"I think he's too little and scared to be any help. Let's see if we can find his parents." We made the turn from the top of the stairs, walking down the short hallway that led to the grand entry hall. Derrick was still by Ramon's ashes, speaking to a pair of his vampires.

I stopped as we passed the foot of the stairs because the gargoyle closest to us woke up, half-extending its wings. One second, it was a statue, the next moving. It turned its smushed-looking face toward me. "Uh oh."

"Give me the child." Its voice sounded like pebbles being poured out of a bag. Mr. Whitehaven hadn't said they could speak verbally.

"Are you its mom? Because I think Tase wants its mom." The grinding sound I'd heard earlier, while scanning the place, filled my mind again. It was a lot louder this time, and ended as something large thumped down at the main doors. I kind of didn't want to look away from Smush, but did and discovered the other vampires scattering at the approach of a tiger-sized gargoyle.

This one was black, and actually did have a feline body, with a long tail ending in a spade point. Its wings were folded, and its lionish face was surrounded by a mane of curls. It tramped right over the late Ramon's ashes, heading directly for me.

"I think that's Mommy," Nick said. "Same tail."

"Give me my child, human." Mama Gargoyle's voice sounded nearly human, with just a touch of a grinding tone.

"That was my plan. Um, Tase?" The baby gargoyle didn't move. "Your mom's here. Time to go home."

"What did you do to him?" Mama Gargoyle bared a set of jagged teeth. So Tase was a boy. Good to know. I heard Nick take a deep breath before moving a step ahead of me. Soames slipped between me and Smush, the one at the foot of the stairs.

"Nothing. He was hiding, and he came out and crawled into my hair."

Leglin suddenly stepped in front of all three of us, and growled at Mama Gargoyle. "*My mistress stated her intentions. She wishes to return the child to you. She does not harm the young or helpless.*"

Mama Gargoyle's tail lashed from side to side, narrowly missing the stomach of one of the vampires as he plastered himself against the wall. She'd understood the hound. "Then surrender him to me."

"I'm trying to. He's scared and won't let go." I lifted my hair so that she could see him. *Tase, you have to go to your mommy. She's getting really mad.*

"Did you touch him?"

"Uh, yeah, but he touched me first. I told you he crawled into my hair, and you can see he's on my neck."

Mama Gargoyle hissed, her too-large eyes becoming slits. Leglin lowered his head and flattened his ears, the fur down his back rising as he bared his teeth in a silent snarl. Crap, we were going to have a fight if we couldn't calm her down.

"Look, I only touched him because he was already touching me, and he's scared. If I'd hurt him, do you think he'd be clinging to my neck like this?" Her eyes became a bit less slitty. "I brought him up here to find you. I don't know why he won't let go. Maybe he thinks he's in trouble."

Her tail slowed its lashing, and she opened her eyes more. Leglin lifted his head an inch, his lips dropping and ears relaxing. All of which seemed good signs. "Maybe if I get closer to you, he'll let go?"

Nick shook his head. "I don't think that's a good idea, Cordi. She could flatten you with one swipe."

"She wants her baby back, and I want to give him back to her. Nobody has to get hurt, right, Mrs...um, ma'am?" A little courtesy couldn't hurt, considering Mama Gargoyle could take off my head with one bite.

She cocked her head, and to my surprise, sat down. "You may approach. I will not harm you."

"Thank you." I stepped to the clear side of Leglin to avoid going around Nick. My hound walked forward with me, halting in front of Mama Gargoyle. Once close, I wasn't sure what to do next. After a second, I pushed my hair over my shoulder and leaned toward her. "Your mommy's right here, Tase."

She cooed wordlessly, startling me. I felt Tase move, his head turning, and winced as he took off. I had a good look as he paused and glanced back, before burying himself in her mane, and he did look like a tiny, cute version of his mom. Backing away, I said, "There you go. Safe and sound."

"We will speak in the future," Mama Gargoyle said as she stood. She turned and tramped back out, mashing vampire ashes deeper into the runner, and took flight just beyond the doors.

"Whew." I turned, noticing Smush had turned to stone again. "That was interesting."

"Yeah, because now you have a gargoyle pissed off at you." Nick frowned, watching the doorway.

"She said 'speak', not 'I'll be back to rip you to shreds'." Soames rotated his head, popping his neck. A grin spread across his face. "That was pretty cool."

"Right?" I giggled, partly from relief. "I didn't even know they were real, and now I've talked to three."

Six

Stone had bagged Gia's earrings, and handed those and Ramon's signet ring over when he rejoined us. I let Derrick see them, but told him, "I'm keeping hold of this evidence for now."

"Of course." His easy agreement surprised me.

"Thanks." I hesitated, looking around. His team appeared to be finishing up, the hum of a small vacuum filling the air as one of them took care of the ashes. "Who was that one?"

"If Ramon and Gia were downstairs, then that victim was Deborah."

"Noted. I think we'll head back to the office. I want to organize the information we have before taking a look at the other scenes."

"Sensible. I'll send photos and information sheets about these three." Derrick held up one of our business cards. "Do I use this email address?"

"Yes, thanks. We'll be back Monday night, to view the other scenes. I'll let you know if anything pops up before then."

Derrick inclined his head, a small smile on his face. "I appreciate your professionalism, Miss Jones."

I nodded back, pleased I'd been able to maintain said professionalism surrounded by so many vampires. Turning away, I waved the guys and Leglin over. "Let's head back to the office."

I let the boss know we were there before leading the guys to what Kate liked to call the War Room. It was a conference room at the opposite end of the building from Mr. Whitehaven's office, roughly the same size, but completely windowless. Custom-made whiteboards were mounted on each wall, stark against the *café au lait* colored paint as they formed a solid strip around the room, broken only by the door. Even their frames were white.

Between those and the long, mahogany table surrounded by matching chairs with dark chocolate leather seats and backrests, I felt slightly intimidated. I'd never used the room before, none of my previous cases being particularly complicated by loads of information. Not that I'd let a silly feeling like that stop me, especially after Derrick's little remarks. Nope, I marshaled my troops, all two of them that possessed thumbs. "We need tape and dry erase markers. We'll file one folder, keep one on hand, and use the third for our case wall."

Soames dropped his folder onto the table. Nick tapped his against his leg. "I'll file mine and get the other stuff from the supply closet."

"Thanks." I opened my folder and lay it on the table to begin sorting the contents as Nick left the room. "I'll put the head shots and info sheets in order of death. Will you separate out the photos for me?"

"Sure." Soames took the stack of photos, each of which had a victim's name at top. Nick returned, bearing the tape and markers, a few minutes before we'd finished.

About an hour passed before everything was arranged to my satisfaction. I wrote the names of the three new victims under those of Lady Esme and her two "favorites", in order of discovery.

We lined up to lean against the table and look over our handiwork. I crossed my arms. "Nine murders, six of them from a single family."

"Which, if Stone knows what he was talking about, means Esme's bloodline is completely wiped out." Nick rubbed his chin.

"How? Someone had to turn her into a vampire."

"Yeah, but she was a master vamp. When a vampire becomes a master, he or she also becomes the beginning of a new bloodline."

"Oh." I learned something new every day. Or in this case, every night. "Don't all vampires eventually become masters?"

"No, not even most of them do. The majority stay minions to their masters forever."

"Bet that sucks." My gaze dropped to Ramon's name. "They do have to be masters to hold council seats, right?"

"Yeah."

"Then if Ramon was her heir apparent, he was a master. Why was he still with her?"

Soames jumped in to answer. "There's levels of mastery too, but even if he was as powerful as Esme, he may have stayed out of loyalty, or even love, if she'd never treated him badly."

"Okay." Love? Not a word I'd use in regard to vampires, because it didn't sit well with me. It wasn't worth wasting time on discussing though. "Back to the bloodline wiped out thing. That sounds personal rather than political to me."

"It could be both." Nick shrugged. "Doesn't really matter since both masters of her line are dead. She wasn't the only council member killed, just the first one."

"Right." I dropped my arms. "Well, I'm going to check email, download and print the pictures we took, and then head home. Why don't you drive Soames home? I'll be ready at ten tomorrow."

"Sure." He kissed my cheek. "Tomorrow will be fun. I promise."

I was finally going to meet his parents, which didn't really fall under "fun" in my thinking, but I smiled anyway. "Yeah. We'll pick you up Monday, Soames. I'll call and let you know when."

"All right. Good night."

After waving them out, I went to my office and logged onto my computer. No email yet. I plugged in my phone after digging it out of my purse, and started the picture file transfer. Next step was hunting down photo paper for my printer.

By the time I had the tray loaded, all the images had transferred to the computer. Unplugging my phone, I dropped it back into my purse and began setting up the printing process. It wasn't until I'd carried the photos to the War Room and began taping them in place that I noticed a defect in one. "Crap."

There was a horizontal blur to the left of the first victim's ashes. I checked the others, wondering if I'd touched the tiny lens on my phone, but they were all fine. Squinting at the blur, I decided it could be Stone's shadow. He'd been standing in the right place when I snapped the first picture.

Minor mystery solved. I rolled my eyes at myself and finished the task before stepping back. I hoped the results looked professional as a thrill of excitement coursed through me. Vampires or not, this was a big case. One closer to those I'd helped the police with, instead of those that typically strolled through the doors of Arcane Solutions.

The excitement faded as I looked at Merriven's section. Regardless of what Derrick thought, Merriven stuck out like a sore thumb to me.

I believed what Ginger had told me about the vamp, that he'd killed humans. Maybe he'd been able to keep that a secret from Derrick and his no-kill buddies, but other vampires with no problem eating people had known his secret. So why would he end up on the hit list, if he was really on the "kill humans" side?

No answer came to mind. I looked at the sections that also only had one victim, wondering if they had the same secret. Maybe, maybe not. It was definitely something to find out. If they did, it would certainly change who the possible suspects were.

Hey, maybe Esme found out Merriven's secret, and told Ramon. Only she'd been killed before they could do anything, and then Ramon went vengeful, killed Merriven and the other two.

I snorted. Holes, there were many in that theory. After all, Lira had been killed after Esme, but before Dalton, and the last three of Esme's bloodline were now kaput too.

They didn't kill themselves just to give me something to do.

Though beginning to feel the effect of my long day, I walked down the wall, double-checking how each had been killed. That was actually pretty easy to determine, something I'd been surprised to learn in the early days of my career.

All of Esme's family had been beheaded, Merriven too, but the other two victims had been staked.

At about a hundred years of age, vampires turned to ash when killed. What kind of ash told you how they'd died. If you burned a vamp, either with fire or sunlight, the ashes were a fine, light gray powder. Quite similar to the ashes you got if you burned a sheet of notebook paper.

Stake one through the heart, and the results looked like fireplace ashes. Some fine powder mixed with heavier gray and black grit, and small charred chunks. Only the chunks were bone, not wood. Lastly, beheading one left behind a sandy black grit that felt greasy.

I glanced at the table and realized no one had carried the sword in from Nick's truck. "Argh."

The jewelry was in my purse. I dug out the two baggies and put them on the table, intending to try psychometry on them come Monday.

We had one murder weapon, but something else had taken off the heads of the last three victims, which meant a total of three different types of weapons were used. That could mean one killer who liked to mix things up, or multiple killers.

The killers could be anyone. Vampires weren't the only supes who favored old-school weaponry. I'd seen both Logan and Nick use swords, as well as Thorandryll and my boss.

The occasional pile of vamp ash would be discovered around the city, leading to rumors of a vigilante group on the prowl. If there really was such a group, they could be humans.

Or psychics.

A few of those piles might've been caused by me, except I tended to use my pyrokinetic ability, leaving the finer, light gray ash behind any vamps who decided to jump me. That stuff seldom ended up in a neat pile, what with the death gyrations. Any that did pile up could be scattered by the lightest of breezes.

Of course, I wasn't the only psychic in town. Just the only one with more than one or two abilities. I grabbed a dry erase marker and moved to a clean white board to make a list of potential suspects.

My job was the find the real killer or killers, not to point fingers at Derrick's political opponents to make things easier for him.

I hesitated before adding "psychics" to the list. Turning vampires over to vampires was one thing, but humans? Shifters or elves?

That would be a problem, since I felt certain vamps didn't have a prison system offering three squares a day, exercise time, and a work program. "I'll cross that bridge if I come to it."

Decided, I capped the marker and stepped back to check my list. Vamps of either party, shifters, elves, the rumored vigilante group, and psychics. After a second, I added one more to the list: humans. Some teen's family could've gone proactive or on a revenge bender.

Fully satisfied I'd covered all potential suspect bases, I left the marker on the table, grabbed my purse, and left the War Room, locking the door behind me. Once in the hall, I called Leglin out of my office, and off the giant doggy bed I kept in there for him. "Let's go home."

Seven

Thanks to a muddled nightmare that included a rotting Ginger, Henry Wilkins' flashing straight razor, and a zombified Dalsarin riding Apep, Eater of Souls, as they chased me through tunnels spewing blood from fanged mouths, my sleep wasn't particularly restful.

They cornered me, and my eyes popped open as Apep began to strike. I barely managed to swallow the scream burning in my throat while focusing on the four dog noses inches from my face. My voice was hoarse. "Guys, come on. We've talked about dog breath first thing in the morning."

"Were you chasing rabbits?" Bone tilted his head more. The other three drew their muzzles back and jumped off the bed. *"You sure were running and whimpering."*

"No, I was being chased." I turned my head to check the time, only to sit upright in a panic. "Crap! I overslept. Move, move!"

I had forty-two minutes before Nick was supposed to arrive, and spent seven of them apologizing and soothing Speck after dumping him off the bed with the covers when I threw them off. He'd tucked in between the top sheet and comforter, and was so light, I hadn't realized he was in them.

Even so, I slid on a pair of red deck shoes at the same time the doorbell rang.

"Nick's here!" Tonya yelled over the thunder of tiny paws—how such small dogs made so much noise running was a mystery to me—and the shrilling chorus of their welcome-slash-warning.

"Thanks! I'll be out in a minute!" I yelled back, giving myself a final once-over in the full-length mirror mounted on the back of my bedroom door. My choice for the day was dark denim capris, the red deck shoes, and a red, short-sleeved polo. Cute, but suitable for light hiking. Nick had told me we'd have to do some walking to reach the village. I hoped the village didn't prove to be of the primitive type. Grabbing my purse and a dark blue, zip-up hoodie, I rushed to the living room. "Hi."

Nick wore a baby blue tee, jeans, and black running shoes. Plus a big smile that made his chocolaty brown eyes appear to twinkle. "Hi. Are you ready?"

"Yes." Not that we were allowed to leave right away. Mom came to tell him hello, and she shoved a large, Halloween-themed tin into my arms.

"There's four dozen peanut butter cookies in there. Nick's favorites." She beamed at him.

"Thanks, Sunny. That was nice of you."

"No problem. You two have a nice day." She waved us out, but not before I pecked her on the cheek.

Outside, Nick helped me into his truck. "How did the pictures come out?"

"Pretty good." I was smiling. He was in a great mood, a combination of happiness and pleasure flowing heavily from him. I soaked it in, letting it flush the dregs of my freaky nightmare away, and we were off.

The entrance to his pack's territory looked a lot like the drive to leading to the house I wanted, just five miles past it and on the opposite side of the highway. The turn-off was nearly hidden by mesquite trees and overgrown brush, but the drive itself was graveled and well-maintained.

It was also an S curve, blocking the view of a small parking area where two neat lines of vehicles sat. The only two openings to the rectangular space were the drive and a dark gray, moss-encrusted stone arch. The day was a lot darker through the arch, because it opened onto a forest. "Not sure I'm ever going to get used to pocket realms."

"They made things a lot easier after the Melding, since most of us weren't displacing human property." Nick guided his truck into the first line of vehicles. "You're going to like this. Our territory's beautiful."

"I bet." Actually, I thought the forest looked spooky. All those trees...anything could be hiding in there. Like a huge pack of wolves.

I followed Nick out, almost forgetting the tin of cookies, and wished Leglin could've come with me. It would've been rude to ask, considering the general dislike and fear most shifters felt toward elf hounds. Plus, probably uncomfortable for Leglin and possibly a sign of distrust, which wouldn't make this visit any more auspicious.

Not that I was expecting it to be easy. This was not a normal "meet the parents" deal. It couldn't be when the parents were shifters and my boyfriend had a ring in waiting.

"Well, come on." Nick took the cookie tin and led the way to the stone arch. The temperature dropped a good ten degrees when I followed him through it. The smell of sun-baked dirt, mesquite, and dryness became cool, pine freshness. I drew in a deep breath, even as a shiver tickled down my back. "Mm."

"Pretty neat, huh?"

"Yeah." Also cooler than I'd expected, so I put on my hoodie as we set off down a rather broad dirt path. It only took a few steps before the feeling of being watched raised the fine hairs on the back of my neck. I didn't see anyone upon casually looking around.

It'd make sense there'd be guards, keeping an eye on the way in, so I did my best to ignore the sensation. I had permission to be here. Now that I was, I could probably teleport in whenever I wanted to. I'd been able to teleport into Thorandryll's fairy mound. No, Logan had told me it was called a sidhe. Anyway, I could teleport into the Barrows too, but tended to use conventional entry methods because appearing smack dab in the middle of vampires made my stomach clench.

We only walked for about five minutes before a trio of people appeared further down the path. One was carrying a toddler. The man in the lead waved at us, and Nick waved back. "That's my dad and mom."

"Oh. Cool." We met halfway between our respective points, and his dad took immediate charge.

"Keith Maxwell, Alpha of the Three Rocks Pack. Call me Keith." He didn't offer his hand. "My mate, Annie."

"Discord Jones. Pleased to meet you both." I wondered who the woman holding the toddler was.

Keith half-turned. "Our grandson, Jake. He's Patrick's first born."

I gave the kid a little wave and smile before meeting the woman's eyes, even though my assessment of Patrick had just taken another deep plunge. "I bet you're his mom."

"Susan," she responded, her tone rather subdued. Keith moved, blocking my view of her.

"I thought we'd take a short walk before lunch, show you around a little."

"Sure." Patrick appeared on the path several feet behind them. He ambled up, took Jake from Susan, and apparently dismissed her since she turned and walked away.

"Psychic Girl finally made it." He nuzzled his son's cheek. "Look, Jake, that's a human." He grinned. "He's never seen one before."

"Cordi's a supe too," Nick said, catching hold of my hand.

"Yeah, but I bet she thinks of herself as human. Don't you?"

"I'm fond of 'person'."

"All over the dog thing?"

"I can still talk to them."

"Pity. Did you keep those yappy little fur balls?"

"One. My mom's keeping the others since they haven't been claimed." I smiled, wondering why he was asking. "And the three ex-fighters are still with me."

He snorted. "The ugly trio."

"That's my pack you're talking about."

"Told you," Patrick said, apparently to his father.

"Accommodations can be made."

What the hell did he mean by that? I glanced at Nick, but Keith turned to walk away and everyone followed him. Nick's mom and brother stepped aside to let us pass, closing ranks behind us.

"We have a large territory. It'd be impossible to cover it all in one day, but I'd like to show you a few spots. We have a lake near the main village."

"Cool." I sensed amusement emanating from Patrick, and didn't think it was from the raspberries he was blowing on his son's chubby little cheek, even though they caused gurgles of laughter from the toddler.

Keith spent the ten minutes it took to reach the lake shore detailing the wild life, deposits of minerals, precious stones, and metals. We walked along the shore, and I could see houses about a half mile around. "That's the main village?"

"Yes. We only have a few hundred of the pack there. The rest are spread among five other villages." He turned away from the lake, leading us to a clearing a few feet into the trees. "What do you think of this view?"

"It's beautiful." It was, standing in the shade of a cypress, looking back at the lake.

"I'm glad you like it. This is the site I've chosen for Nick's future home. It's far enough from the village your dogs won't disturb anyone, and they'll have some room to run." He turned around, pointing to a spot to the left of the clearing. "We can build a pen for them there, since they'll need to be put up at night."

What in the hell? I noticed Patrick's grin and tried to keep my tone polite. "My dogs live in the house."

Keith frowned. "Interesting. We may have to build something a bit larger then, if Nick doesn't mind them sharing your home."

The picture forming in my head of what it'd be like to live here wasn't a pleasant one. As a guest, I didn't want to be rude, but couldn't keep from saying, "You're planning a little far ahead for me."

Keith smiled. "It's no trouble. The house will be a wedding gift from the pack."

There had to be a wedding for there to be wedding gifts. I bit my tongue, determined not to make a scene. Nick and I were so going to have a long talk later, though. "Generous."

Patrick laughed, lifting Jake to blow a raspberry on the kid's stomach. I glanced at their mother. She hadn't said a word yet, and it didn't appear she felt a need to join the conversation.

"I make certain everyone has what they need, especially newly mated couples." Keith waved for us to follow him as he began walking again. "No one should have to begin their pairing with worries about housing and such."

Oh, yes, Nick and I were going to have a long, long talk later.

By the time we reached the village, I was seriously considering faking a sudden illness. Keith had rambled the whole walk over, mostly humble bragging about what a great pack leader he was.

"And of course, all requests to come and go require my permission," he said, halting to throw his arm out in a grand gesture. "Our main village."

"It's lovely," I replied, and it really was. All of the houses I could see were solid-looking log cabins of the sort a high-end mountain resort might have. Even the roofs were shingled in wood. No paint to be seen, though some did have a little stone work for variety. Nor had everyone used the same woods, resulting in a subdued, but pretty, wooden rainbow. Like most human homes, each had grass yards, with trees, shrubbery, or flowers for decoration.

Looking around, I felt a mad desire to go shopping for pink flamingo and garden gnome lawn ornaments. I could do a midnight visit, plant one of each in every yard.

The place was just a little too picture perfect. Also, really quiet. "Where is everyone?"

"I wanted your first visit to be with just us. They're out and about, busy with patrols and other things."

"Oh." Wow, had he really shooed a couple hundred people out of their homes? I suddenly knew exactly where Patrick had gotten his massive ego from.

"Why don't you go help Susan with lunch?"

I thought Keith meant me until Annie nodded. She had yet to say a word.

"Cordi's mom sent cookies." Nick gave his mother the tin and a bright smile. She returned it, offered me a slight nod, and walked off. I watched her climb the steps of the largest, two-story cabin.

"I should go help with lunch."

Keith wasn't about to let me escape. "Of course not. Today, you're a guest." He pointed. "Over there is the path that leads to our ceremonial ground. That's where you and Nick will be married."

I couldn't stand it anymore. "If we get married."

He completely ignored that. "After lunch, we'll walk there and then to the waterfall."

I tuned him out, nodding and making polite noises as required right up until we finally went in for lunch.

Annie and Susan bustled back and forth from the kitchen to dining room, setting the table and bringing out food. The furnishings suited the woodsy setting, all wood, leather, and dark-colored fabrics. Everything had that beautiful, understated look of plain but fantastic craftsmanship.

Desperate to stop Keith's steady droning, I asked Patrick to let me hold Jake, and made the mistake of saying, "I love kids."

Keith jumped right on that as Patrick, still grinning widely, handed over the toddler. "You should have several then."

I settled Jake on my lap and sniffed his golden curls. He smelled like clean baby and sunshine. "I love other people's kids. You can give them back after a little bit."

"Cordi's not sure she wants kids," Nick said, handing me a bread roll. "Here, he likes these."

"You do." The way Keith said it made it clear he thought that was all that mattered. "She'll need something to fill her days with."

Oh my God, he didn't just...I didn't look up, and the only reason my tone stayed pleasant was because of the kid in my lap. "I have a job. My days are pretty full."

"Oh, you won't need to keep it. It's the man's duty to put food on the table."

Teeth gritted, I made as non-committal a sound as possible, aware of Patrick's amusement turning into outright glee. It took me a few seconds to realize he was waiting for me to blow up at his dad.

Not about to indulge him, or be a less-than-courteous guest, I fed Jake the roll and reconsidered pretending a sudden illness.

That idea was looking so much better every passing minute.

Much, much later, I said, "That's okay. It's late. I'll teleport home."

"Well," Nick glanced at his dad. "Okay."

I turned to Keith and Annie. Susan had disappeared after dinner. Neither of the women had eaten with us. "Thank you for having me over. It was fun," I lied through my teeth with that one. "The food was great, and Jake's a sweetheart."

"You're quite welcome. Next time, we'll barbecue and have everyone here," Keith promised.

I could only imagine what a party that would be. "Sounds fun."

Annie just smiled. She had two expressions: Smiling or solemn.

Turning back to Nick, I said, "See you Monday. Good night."

"Night." We exchanged a chaste kiss and I teleported the hell out of there, straight to Mom's kitchen. Opening the fridge, I pulled out a wine cooler and gulped it down. "Ah."

My God, Keith loved the sound of his own voice. Maybe Annie didn't talk because she couldn't get a word in edgewise. From what I'd seen, Nick's pack appeared to be stuck somewhere in oh, say, the fifties. Possibly the eighteen-fifties.

Women kept house, cooked, had babies, and raised them. At least they did the girl babies. I wasn't certain they were allowed such an important job as raising the sons. With a shudder, I grabbed another wine cooler. After dropping my empty into the trash, I walked to my room, sipping at the second cooler.

If I did eventually marry Nick, there was no way in hell we'd live in his father's domain. No way, no how would I subject myself to living under Keith's thumb, having my life dictated to me on a daily basis.

The miracle was that Nick wasn't a mirror image of him. Maybe Annie had something to do with that? I could see Keith "allowing" her more influence over their younger son. After all, Patrick was his heir.

Yep, Keith behaved exactly as I'd expect a Dark Ages king to. "Ugh."

I went to bed, wondering how to let Nick know that I didn't want to be around his dad again. That wasn't exactly an easy thing to tell your boyfriend.

Eight

At nine-thirty AM sharp, I teleported to the door of Logan's apartment and knocked. I heard Terra yell, "Discord's here!" before she ran to open the door. "Hi!"

"Hey. Mom's already baking cookies. I like your tee." It was cotton candy pink and said "Keep Calm and Have Some Bacon".

She grinned. "Logan's...."

"Ready," he said, exiting his bedroom while tucking in the back of his shirt. His tee didn't say anything, but the forest green color looked great on him, and fit snugly enough to do a little muscle showcasing. It wasn't tight enough to show off the six-pack I felt certain he had. I hadn't looked that far down the one surprise opportunity I'd had to do so.

"Awesome, come on." Stepping back to give them room to join me in the hallway, I held out my hands. Once they'd taken hold, I teleported us home, to the living room. By pre-arrangement, it was empty but didn't stay that way long. Shrill barking heralded the arrival of the Chihuahua Brigade, basically shouting what translated to *The nice animal people are here!*

I laughed. "They like you guys."

Terra squatted down, trying to pet each little round skull as the dogs pushed and shoved each other. Logan bent to scoop up two: Speck and a kind of brindled little female who followed Speck around in order to boss him. I'd named her "Squishy" because she was slightly overweight and felt squishy.

"I thought you must be back," Mom said, holding the swinging door to the kitchen open. "Good morning."

"Morning, Sunny." Logan smiled at her while his cousin hastily stood.

"Hi, Mrs. Jones."

"Call me Sunny. I have fresh cookies waiting to be gobbled in here." She let the door go, disappearing from sight.

"With a mountain of work right behind them," I whispered before heading toward the kitchen. The two shifters followed, Chihuahuas dancing and prancing and generally making walking an interesting adventure.

"Where are the big dogs?" I asked, noticing they weren't in the kitchen.

"Back yard with Tonya. Here." Mom handed over a plate of warm, chocolate chip cookies. "Have a few and then we'll get things set up. I have milk, coffee, tea, or soda. Which do you want?"

Twenty minutes later, and more than a few cookies consumed, we moved to the dining room. Boxes stood stacked along the two longer walls, and Mom had already set up a second, long table next to the dining table. A stack of dark purple gift bags waited at the end of one table, near the windows looking out over the back yard. I could see Red and Bone wrestling over a tug o' war toy rope, while Diablo snoozed in a patch of sunlight.

Mom handed out box cutters. "Open one box from each stack, so that I can decide where each goes."

It didn't take long to set up the assembly line. Long familiar with Mom's methods, I grabbed a gift bag and opened it while Mom and Tonya set up a card table. "We start here, and just work our way around the table, putting one of each thing in the bags, and then hand the bags off to Mom or Tonya. They'll line them up against the wall after they do the finishing touches."

"We're going to run out of room fast," Terra said, picking up a gift bag.

"We'll load the cars and transfer them to the center once we have full loads." Smiling, Mom waved a package of orange gift tissue paper and a spool of inch-wide, white ribbon decorated with a conga line of ghosts and skeletons. "All right, go team!"

I made another round of the table, Terra and Logan following, before Mom asked, "So how was yesterday?"

The instant scowl on my face raised her eyebrows. I forced my scowl away. "Um, interesting?" Noticing the two shifters looking at me, I added, "I met Nick's parents and spent the day with them."

"You say 'interesting', but your face said something way different," Tonya said, tying a bow on the handles of a bag.

"His dad is a control freak. Would you believe he has a spot picked out to build us a house on? I mean, okay, it's a pretty spot, but still. Who does that?" Before anyone respond, I plunged ahead. "Oh, and get this. He said 'accommodations can be made' for the dogs, and got a big frowny face when I told him they lived inside. Said it would be up to Nick if they did there."

Logan laughed, choking it off when Terra elbowed him in the ribs. "Sorry."

"Why was that funny?"

"It wasn't, but imagining the look on your face while he was talking? That was funny." He coughed, his lips twitching. "What did you say to him?"

"None of the stuff I really wanted to."

His shoulders quivered, and Terra elbowed him again. "Quit laughing."

"I can't." The words were strangled. "I can only imagine what she did say."

I adopted a lofty tone. "Since I was a guest, I was polite."

"We did raise you to be polite, but not to let yourself be pushed around." Mom frowned. "I'm guessing wolf shifter society is patriarchal?"

"You have no idea. The men didn't do jack during meals except eat and talk, and I was the only woman at the table. Nick's mom and Patrick's girlfriend did all the cooking and clean up both times. I think they ate in the kitchen." My scowl had made a comeback. "Nick bragged about my cooking."

Logan had gotten himself under control. "You're a really good cook, so that's not a bad thing, right?"

"It wouldn't be if his dad hadn't acted like that was way more important than my job." I hesitated. "His dad just assumed I'd quit working once we married. You should've seen his face when I said I wasn't going to quit my job for years and years."

"Once you married?" Tonya's eyes were wide, and her brows so high, her bangs hid them. "Um, did Nick tell them something different from what you told us?"

"Oh, no, nothing like that. I think Keith doesn't comprehend the possibility that a woman can resist a marriage proposal. He has everyone's lives planned out. Including mine."

With an exaggerated shudder, she said, "Sounds like he needs a swift kick in the b...."

Mom *tsk*ed, cutting her off. "Now, now. Violence doesn't...."

It was my turn to interrupt. "Did I mention I'd have to ask permission to see you, or to have you come visit?"

Mom's face tightened, her lips thinning. "He told you that? Maybe he does need a swift kick."

That did it. I laughed and flapped my hand at her. "Doesn't matter. Even if I did marry Nick, we wouldn't live there. No way, no how. I'd be too tempted to use my abilities on Keith and Patrick, probably every time they opened their mouths."

Tonya side-eyed me. "But not Nick?"

"I like him." I usually won when we argued, too.

"So you are thinking about marrying him?" Terra didn't look up from her bag stuffing.

"It's like someone telling you not to think of pink elephants. I can't not think about it," I explained.

"Oh."

"You're young and you have plenty of time to decide if you want to marry Nick, someone else, or not marry at all." Mom took the bag I'd finished. "Don't stress over it."

"Good advice, but not so easy to follow. The longer we see each other, the higher the chance he'll think things will go the way he wants." I grabbed another bag. "After yesterday, I'm kind of thinking we should take a break."

No one rushed to tell me that was a great idea. Then again, none of them said it was a bad one either. "Oh, come on. I have the Give Me Advice sign out."

Tonya shook her head. "Not me. I do not give romantic advice to my elders."

"Ouch, way to make me feel old."

She grinned. "I'm unrepentant."

"Brat." I glanced at my mom. "You're up."

She shook her head. "I'm not an expert on shifters, much less young men."

We both looked at Logan, who began stuffing the gift bag he held as though his life depended on it. Terra snorted. "You don't want his advice."

"Why not?"

"Because he'll tell you stuff like 'go with your instincts' and 'you'll know when someone's the right one'. It's not actually helpful."

"That was good advice," Logan protested. "And it'll work, if you use it."

"Right. I told you I liked Devon, and you came back with a list of reasons he's totally inappropriate," she shot back. "One was 'he's a snot-nosed smart ass'."

He shrugged. "He is. Kid's got an ego bigger than our building."

My mom laughed. "Most teenaged boys have large egos, or at least pretend they do. So do most teenaged girls."

"Hey, we resemble that remark," Tonya said, waving her hand between Terra and herself. "At least the teenaged part."

"I said most, not all."

"If yours gets too big, Mom will definitely let you know." I smiled, remembering a few "talks" we'd had. "One of her many talents: Talking down overblown egos."

"Maybe I should send Devon to her," Logan muttered.

Terra glared at him, so I hurried to speak before she let loose. "Would you give me the same advice?"

"What?" Logan blinked. "Oh. No, I'd tell you that wolves have definite opinions about proper behavior. That if you think the two of you argue a lot now, just wait until you tell him you won't live on pack territory. Nick doesn't strike me as the lone wolf type, so he won't go for that." Logan frowned. "Then again, he and I don't get along well, so anything I say, you should probably take with a grain of salt."

"Yeah, right. You only pointed out stuff I've already experienced." I sighed. "You know, being an adult isn't nearly as much fun as I thought it would be."

"It usually isn't," Mom agreed. "I do have a little bit of advice to throw in the pot. Do what feels right for you, and what will make you happy in the long run."

"Wow, I just realized how much you," Terra poked Logan in the side, "sound like a parent."

"Um," he glanced at my mom. "I'll take that as a compliment."

"Good plan," Mom said, her eyes twinkling. "Now, I'm going to switch to boss mode. Let's step up production, people, or we won't finish today."

We stepped up production.

By lunchtime, we'd managed to fill up both cars. Mom called a break. "We'll eat, then Tonya and I will do a delivery run while you three get back to work."

"Aye aye, Captain." I saluted her. "What's for lunch?"

"Chicken and dumplings with sweet cornbread."

"Ooh!" Tonya tied off another bag and stretched. "My favorite."

"Mine too." I hurried to finish the bag I was working on. "Terra, if you and Logan like them, I'll teach you how to make them."

"Cool." Her bright smile caused a flash of guilt. I hadn't exactly kept up with my promise of cooking lessons.

"Maybe next Sunday? Would that work?"

"I know you're busy...."

"I'll come over at four, and we'll make dinner," I promised, trying to remember if they had a DVD player. "I can bring some movies too."

"Awesome." She practically bounced out of the room, a gleeful smile on her face. They were keeping her under wraps big time, if she felt so pleased over my planned visit. I wasn't that exciting of a guest.

Maybe now that I had some time off from house hunting—I hoped, permanently—I could spend more time with her. Maybe take her places. Nothing like teleportation to keep a future Queen's shopping itinerary secret.

Listening to her chatter with Tonya as they served themselves, I decided to include her too, at least as often as possible. The chestnut-haired teen didn't do much beyond helping Mom, working at the Blue Orb, and studying magic with David and Jo.

I noticed Logan looking at me, and grinned. He automatically smiled back, but curiosity surrounded him like a cloud of too-strong cologne.

Time enough later to run the idea past him, and see if he'd agree. Right now, there was food, fun company, and good work to finish.

I even put aside my relationship woes to enjoy the rest of the day.

Nine

On Monday, I picked up Soames before heading to the office. We arrived at three, and there was a new face at the reception desk. A pretty new face topped with burgundy hair. "Welcome to Arcane Solutions. How may I help you?"

"Is Cordi," Percy informed the woman behind the desk. The fact the parrot spoke to her, and nicely, meant that he liked her. "Cordi, this Tabitha."

"Hi." Holy cow, we finally had a new receptionist. Kate had to be overjoyed. "Nice to meet you, Tabitha. This is Soames."

"Oh, hi. Nice to meet you too." She had an infectious grin and twinkly blue eyes. "Nick and Mr. Whitehaven are in the War Room."

"Thanks and welcome aboard."

"Thank you."

I glanced down the hall as we walked past her desk, and saw that Kate's office door was shut. She was either with a client, or on the phone with Alleryn. I'd be planning a night out in celebration if I were her, after months of pulling double duty.

When we went into the War Room, Mr. Whitehaven was studying my list of possible suspects. "Afternoon, guys. Oh good, you remembered the sword."

"I did." Nick smiled, and I pecked him on the cheek while dropping my purse in a chair. I still hadn't decided how to broach the subject of his dad.

"Thanks. I met our new receptionist. She's nice."

Mr. Whitehaven nodded, before indicating my list. "It appears you don't believe the murders are politically motivated."

Crap. My mood plummeted at the idea of having to justify my thoughts on the case. "I want to be certain we consider all possibilities."

"Commendable." With that one word, my spirits were restored. "Have you had any insights?"

He meant psychic ones. "Not yet. I'm going to handle the other two items before we go check out the rest of the scenes."

"Excellent. I'll leave you three to it." With a faint smile, the boss vacated the room. It felt much bigger once he had. The man had presence, not just eight feet of height.

"Okay, let's get busy. Either of you have any thoughts or suggestions?"

"Why did you put shifters on that list?" Nick asked. Soames walked over to read it.

"I listed everyone capable of killing vampires. You did see that I have psychics on there too, right?" So much for not having to justify my thinking.

"If we were after a vampire, we'd wait until they came out. The Barrows is their stronghold, Cordi. No one enters without being noticed." He looked perfectly serious.

"Tourists go down there all the time."

"Yeah, and you can bet half the council knows just how many and what species every single day," he said. I saw Soames nod in agreement from the corner of my eye as he turned away from the white board.

"On the other hand, the Barrows are different from other pocket realms. It's not one single realm, but several stuck together."

I blinked at Soames. There was my new thing learned for the day. Yay. "How does that even...never mind. Okay, so who could get in without being noticed?"

"Vampires, elves, and maybe psychics if they can teleport like you do. Or have some other ability to keep from being noticed." Soames glanced at Nick. "Right?"

"Yes. Probably little folk too, but only to scrounge or steal. Not to murder. Vamps don't prey on them. Not enough blood."

Ugh. I shivered. "Right. Go ahead and edit the list."

Soames did, and I sighed. My possible suspect list was down to four types, and fifty percent were vampires. Oh, well. I sat down and snagged the baggie holding Ramon's ring. The instant it landed in the palm of my hand, a hunger for blood hit me like an impatient mugger. My heart pounded, and I quickly dropped the ring on the table. "I hate that."

"Hate what?" Soames sat down, Nick following suit.

"Vampire belongings, like this stupid ring, have a tendency to soak up their owners' blood thirst." I scrubbed my hand on my jeans. "It's disgusting."

Nick eyed me. "You're not going to try and bite us, are you?"

"I might. The ring has it bad. He must've worn it all the damn time." I scowled at the ring. "Crap. Going in for a second time."

This time, I only touched it with the tip of one finger, not that it helped. Ramon's blood lust raged up my arm, filling my chest with heat, and my mouth with drool. Swallowing, I couldn't help turning my head to look at Soames.

He prudently retreated from his chair, quickly enough to tip it over. The dull thump of it hitting the carpeted floor sounded like a panicked heartbeat. "Um, her eyes."

I could hear both their hearts beating, and a soft rushing sound. Blood.

Nick grabbed my wrist, yanking my hand away from the ring. My neck popped as I quickly turned my head toward him, hissing and baring fangs I didn't have. He hastily let go, backing away with his hands in the air. "Yeah, that's not good."

Muscles tensed, I was a breath away from leaping on him when the realization they were both scared broke through and made me giggle. Nick relaxed, dropping his arms to his sides. "You okay now?"

"Yeah, I think so. Except really thirsty. I'm gonna grab a soda. Please put that damn ring back in the bag. Do either of you want anything?" They didn't, and I left for the break room, muffling giggles the whole way. I managed to stop before returning, but Soames' wary expression nearly set me off again. I took a deep breath. "Did you say something about my eyes?"

"Yeah. They turned red, like a vampire's does when it's hungry."

"Seriously?" I was so going to take the ring to the restroom for a third try, just to see if that would happen again. With Percy as my chaperone. He'd nip if necessary, to shock me out of the blood lust before I went looking for someone to eat.

"Seriously," Nick confirmed. "Guessing the ring's useless?"

"Eh. Something else may have transferred. I'll just have to wait and see." I sat back down and reached for the baggie with the earrings. After taking a sip of my soda, I opened it.

"Ah, should you touch those right now?" Soames had put the table between us.

"Might as well. I doubt she wore them all the time. It shouldn't be as bad."

"Okay, but I'm staying over here."

"What if I go after Nick?"

"I'll pull you off. Carefully. I haven't tussled with many humans. Don't want to accidentally break your arm or something."

Suddenly glad I hadn't teased him with a "Fraidy cat", I nodded. "Right. I forget you guys are stronger. Okay, here we go."

All I needed was one earring. Holding one back, I let the other fall into my hand.

Fear slammed into my head as though someone had slugged me with a baseball bat. I heard a scream, followed by a shout: "Run!"

Darkness and a cool breeze. Burning pain then...nothing.

Shuddering, I dropped the earring back in the baggie. "It remembers her death, but I didn't see who was chasing her. She was terrified."

There were goose bumps on my arms. I rubbed them away. Terror was another emotion I hadn't thought vampires felt.

We had dinner before driving to the Barrows, and I waited to call for Leglin until just before we went down. My hound buddy appeared with a wide grin and wagging tail.

He was obviously enjoying being a part of our investigative team. I suddenly wondered if he'd spent most of his time in a kennel, back when Thorandryll had him.

Stone met us at the foot of the stone steps, with transportation no less: An open air carriage pulled by two solid-black horses. A second vampire sat in the driver's seat. "Nice wheels."

"Lord Derrick's compliments, to lessen the traveling time. Do you wish to view the scenes in order, or begin with the one furthest away from here?"

"Which one is that?"

"Where Lira died."

"Yes, let's start there and then go to where Dalton died."

"As you wish, Miss Jones." Stone offered me his hand, and I realized he had on gloves. The carriage steps looked frail, so I accepted his offer of help getting in.

Nick hopped right up, and we took the front seat, which meant we were facing the back of the carriage. Soames sat across from me, and Stone settled next to him. The four of us took up most of the available leg room, not leaving much for Leglin.

My hound stuck his head in the side of the carriage to look up at me. "*I will run alongside.*"

"Okay." He probably needed the exercise. Mom's backyard wasn't all that big. Tonya took the big dogs down to the closest park every morning, but the park wasn't exactly huge. If I got the house I wanted, space for the dogs to run wouldn't be an issue anymore.

The carriage lurched into motion. Having never ridden in one before, I mentally added it to my bucket list and crossed it right off. My job had added stuff to that list I had no idea I wanted to experience, until the opportunity to do so appeared. Like riding a flying horse. That had been pretty freakin' cool. I looked at Stone. "My associates tell me that no one enters the Barrows unobserved."

"They are correct."

"Then you guys should be able to help close a lot of missing person cases."

He didn't miss a beat. "Their exits aren't as closely observed."

"Right." I drawled the word out. Some "exits" weren't of the voluntarily leaving kind. Even vampires seldom wanted witnesses when they killed. "But there's probably some who could get in without being seen, right?"

"Do you have a point to these questions?"

"Why doesn't anyone ever want to play Twenty Questions with me?" My complaint went unanswered. I huffed. "Yes, I think it may be possible someone other than a vampire could've killed them."

"The evidence indicates otherwise."

"So you're telling me there's no way an elf or psychic could've done it?"

Stone opened his mouth then closed it. I continued. "Wiping out an entire blood line sounds kind of personal to me."

He frowned. "Esme has a surviving child. They didn't part on amiable terms."

Bingo, maybe. "You didn't mention that Friday night. I'll want to question...."

"He's difficult to locate. They parted ways several centuries ago."

My snort raised Stone's eyebrows. "Difficult doesn't mean impossible. But he's not a surviving child, because he's a master, right?"

"He's...not a vampire."

Well, that didn't exactly compute. He was her child, and centuries old, but not a vampire. Wait. "Dhampyr?"

"Yes."

Holy crap, an actual, day-walking bloodsucker. Logan had told me they were for real, but sheesh. "You kind of sidestepped a minute ago. Can dhampyrs not be masters?"

"Not exactly, Miss Jones." Stone looked past me. "We've arrived."

"Good. What do you mean by not exactly?"

"Dhampyrs don't necessarily have all the same attributes or powers as vampires. There's a tradeoff for being able to walk in the sun."

"Little or no psychic abilities?"

Stone nodded, which sort of answered a question I'd never asked: How did vampires become masters? The psychic ability bit looked to play a big part there. "If he's not a master, and not grudgy enough to plot murder, he could be in danger."

The big vamp chuckled. "He could also be in Alaska, for all I know of his current whereabouts."

"Noted. Try and find him anyway, okay?"

"Of course."

With that, we exited the carriage and I looked around. "This isn't an area I've been in before."

No mansions or castles on this street. The buildings were crammed together, and the area highly resembled certain parts of the Palisades. Minus all the graffiti. "I didn't realize vampires would stoop to being slum lords."

Stone's upper lip curled as he looked around. "This is where the masterless and bite junkies live."

Bite junkies were humans addicted to feeding vamps. I hadn't known any actually lived in the Barrows. "Isn't it a bad idea to have those two types living in close quarters?"

"Yes. Cleaning up this area is on the council's agenda. Too high of a PR risk."

"I bet. What was Lira doing here?"

All three of the men stared at me. Nick decided to answer. "Bite junkies are also called blood whores, Cordi."

Trust vampires to pervert the oldest profession in the world. "Oh, but again: What was Lira doing here? She was part of a wealthy family. Why would she be slumming?"

No one had an actual answer. Some suggestions that turned my stomach, yeah, but not firm answers. I threw up my hands to stop their speculation. "Enough. Time's a wastin'."

Lira had died in an alley behind a three-story building. The ground floor was a grocery store, but the top two floors were apartments. Metal stairs led up to walkways that ran the length of the building for each floor. Some of the residents hung out of their windows, or stood on the walkways, watching us.

While Nick and Soames poked around, I used my telepathy to scan for any loud, potentially useful thoughts. If anyone had seen something, they might be too afraid to come forward.

I did pinpoint three witnesses, and with the lightest possible touch, managed to "suggest" to one to recall what he'd seen. He did, and it didn't make the slightest bit of sense.

He saw Lira's head fall off. That was it.

No one swinging a weapon to cut it off. She'd been walking. Then her head just flew off, her body hitting the ground a few seconds later, already beginning to decompose.

I tried my luck with the second witness, but couldn't get her to recall her memory of that night. The third, a woman, had seen the same thing as the man had, from a slightly different angle.

It appeared we needed to put out an APB on the Invisible Man. "Hey, Stone."

"Yes?"

"Did anyone bother to scan for witnesses?" Most vampires had telepathy, which I felt was really unfair.

"Of course. No one saw anything useful."

"Yeah, seeing her head suddenly go flying, not remotely useful."

He sighed. "They didn't see the killer. That would've been useful, Miss Jones."

I felt like face palming. "And the fact they didn't isn't useful? Are you kidding me? He may have altered their memories, wiped himself out of them."

The big vamp frowned before conceding, "It's possible."

Disbelief shrilled my voice. "You think? Well, think about this too: Someone capable of selectively altering memories might also be able to unalter them."

His eyes widened and his lips parted. "You're right." He pulled out his cell phone. "I'll pass that on to my master."

"Yeah, do that." Did we need to check the other scenes now? I debated while he made the call. There was something I wanted to check into concerning the other two council members. Plus, it could take a while to undelete the witnesses' memories, if anything actually had been deleted from them.

A nagging sensation that I'd forgotten something important

struck, but try as I might, I couldn't think of what it might be.

"Your insight just now may very well have solved the case," Stone said, putting the brakes on my effort to remember. "Do you still wish to see the other scenes?"

"We can skip Dalton's, but I do want to visit the other two." With the lead I'd given them, Derrick would follow through with any witnesses to Dalton's murder.

"As you wish."

I spent the carriage ride to our next stop patting myself on the back. In spite of being a baby compared to vampires when it came to psychic abilities, I'd come up with something that hadn't crossed their minds.

Discord Jones, 1. Vampires, 0.

"Lord Holmesby's remains were discovered by a Lady Serena. They had a thing," Nick said after checking the folder. "Downstairs, second level."

"Okay. Stone, would you mind taking Soames down for a look? I want to get a feel for the place. I could have a retrocog if it's quiet enough."

"Certainly."

As soon as they were gone from view, I turned to Nick. "I need you and Leglin to start sniffing around."

"For what?"

"Dead bodies."

Nick scrunched up his face. "Come again?"

"Publicly, Merriven was all 'no killee the humans' but privately was a different story. I want to know if Holmesby had the same private activities."

"Okay, but it'll take hours to cover this whole place. Even if Holmesby did kill, he didn't necessarily hide the bodies here."

True. I looked at Leglin, trying to think of a way to speed up the search. The hound stared back, his ears perked. When an idea surfaced, my resulting grin must've been pretty mischievous looking, from the way Nick's eyes narrowed. "What?"

"Leglin, any chance you could maybe talk some of your pack mates into helping out?"

My boyfriend's eyes went wide. "You're going to steal Prince Jerk-Off's hounds?"

"Not steal, borrow. What do you think, buddy?"

"*I will ask.*" Leglin disappeared.

Nick scowled. "If Thorandryll notices they're gone, he's going to demand payment. He already has you on the hook for a date."

"I'll swear them to secrecy."

He grunted. "Good luck with that."

"I'll guilt him into letting it slide." After all, it was the prince's fault the lone surviving dark elf had attacked Santo Trueno. Said dark elf had shot me in the shoulder with a freaking arrow. "I did spill blood for him again, and I'm no more one of his people than I was when he sicced those demons on me."

My boyfriend considered that for a few seconds. "True, but his healer fixed you up."

"Different elf, different deal." I hoped. Alleryn hadn't ever asked me for anything. His fee through the hospital had been paid though. Did that make us even?

I dismissed worrying about it when Leglin reappeared, with about two dozen other hounds. "Wow. Good job."

My hound lowered his head, his ears drooping. "*I promised each a steak as payment.*"

Ouch. That was going to dent the hell out of my budget. "Sure. We'll have a cookout and they can all come."

Tails wagged, creating a surprising air draft, and the hounds took off. Some trotted or ran, others simply disappeared. It was unnerving to know they were there, yet not hear anything. I looked at Nick. "Do you think Stone will freak?"

"Duh."

Too late to worry about it. The big problem would be getting them from here to the last scene.

Leglin reappeared. "*The top floors are clear.*"

"Cool. Um, you did them not to attack anyone, right?"

"*Of course, mistress.*"

"Fantastic. Carry on." I blinked and he was gone again. "I need to get him a girlfriend. They could have puppies, and then I'd have my own pack of elf hounds. How cool would that be?"

"Not very. My dad wouldn't let them all on pack territory."

Crap, I had yet to talk to him about that. "Yeah, about that...."

"Miss Jones!" Stone's yell echoed through the great hall.

Oops.

We stood in a circle around a giant, iron-bound, wooden well cap. "Looks like I was right to play that hunch."

"We'll see." Stone's frosty rejoinder had me hiding a grin. One of the hounds swore he could smell dead bodies on the other side of the well cap. I was inclined to believe him simply because of how well hidden the room had been. I glanced at the door. We'd had to crawl through a wardrobe in Holmesby's bedchamber to get here.

"One of these days, I'll find a wardrobe that leads to Narnia."

"And Aslan will make you a queen," Soames said. We traded a smile. Obviously, Logan wasn't the only person in his clan with a library card and no fear of using it.

"Who's Aslan?"

Stone answered Nick. "The lion in 'The Lion, the Witch, and the Wardrobe'. Let's move this cap, gentlemen."

"I can give you guys a TK boost if you need any extra help." Retreating to the doorway, I watched as they selected handholds.

"One, two, three." They strained, but no dice. Stone growled. "Again."

I helped with a push of telekinesis, only to wish I hadn't as the giant lid flipped over, releasing a stench worse than anything the morgue or city dump had on offer.

My stomach heaved, and it wasn't the only one. Everyone threw up.

Even Stone, and it wasn't blood coming out of him.

"You're not a vampire." We'd retreated to Lord Holmesby's drawing room to rinse out our mouths with brandy, it being the only thing readily available. "You're not human either. You're a dhampyr, aren't you?"

Stone grimaced, took another slug of brandy to swish around, and spat it out into the empty fireplace. "Yes. Lord Derrick is my father."

"Oh." Not my wittiest response, probably because I couldn't get the smell/taste combo out of the back of my throat. "Better call him."

"I will, after we've searched the Tanaka estate." The dhampyr downed the last of his brandy. "I hope to God we don't make a similar discovery."

"If we do, someone else can open it," Nick said. "I'm damn sure not going to. Not after that."

"Me neither." Soames shuddered, his eyes still watering. "That was incredibly putrid."

"Yeah, it was." I buried my nose in my glass, hoping the brandy's aroma would overpower the "mass grave with a side of vomit" still lingering between my nose and the back of my tongue. It didn't. I downed the brandy. "All right, let's hit the road."

Ten

One elf hound made vampires clear the way. A herd of elf hounds could empty streets.

Vampires blurred away at top speed, ducking into buildings or even climbing them as we went, until all I could hear was the clip clop of the horses' hooves.

It was funny, but I didn't laugh because of Nick. His furrowed brow and side-glances made it clear he hadn't forgotten what I'd said before we were interrupted earlier. At least he wasn't bringing it up now. Maybe I'd have a brainstorm about what to say before he did.

Or maybe I should admit there wasn't a future for an "us" since I couldn't see one that didn't include me having to give up basically everything.

That would be the adult thing to do. But it was nice having a boyfriend who wasn't scared off by my psychic abilities. Mentally shaking my head, I refocused on the case.

We now had two murder victims who'd pretended to be good little vamps. Exactly how did they fit in the puzzle? "We should check Esme's estate too."

"That won't be necessary. The gargoyles wouldn't be there." Stone leaned forward, resting his forearms on his knees. He was behaving more human since upchucking. "They were originally created to protect humans. She wouldn't have been able to claim the loyalty of so many if she, or any of her family, were routinely draining humans."

I glanced at Soames for confirmation, and received a slight nod. "Okay, we'll leave her and her family marked as good guys then. I bet if we have the hounds search Merriven's estate, we'll find more bodies."

The dhampyr leaned back. "Would they obey someone else?"

I put the question to Leglin, and after a few minutes of discussion, we dropped off him, Soames, and a dozen hounds to search Merriven's estate when we passed by it. Another hound, named Enid, stepped forward to take charge of those left.

Lord Tanaka's estate was a graceless pile of volcanic rock, but the inside was Japanese themed. I spent the time the hounds were searching admiring a collection of weapons, armor, dragon statues, and of all things, dried flowers mounted in picture frames.

Soames called me. "No bodies, but there's a room on the second floor that's suspicious. The hounds are going nuts, but I don't know why. I can't smell anything, and there aren't any blood stains."

"Okay, take pictures of it, grab Leglin's collar when you're done, and tell him to bring everyone to me."

"Will do." We ended the call and Enid popped into view.

"*We've found what you seek.*"

"Thank you. Will you show us?"

She assented, her head and tail held high, and led the way at a deliberate pace. Elf hounds could really pile on the dignity when they wanted to.

Tanaka had a disposal pit hidden behind a solid iron door on the lowest basement level. It wasn't far from his personal chambers. We held our breath while opening the door, but it didn't smell like Holmesby's well had. I pointed to the bags of quicklime stacked in a corner. "That keeps the bodies from smelling, but contrary to popular belief, it also does a pretty good job of preserving them."

"I think I'll inform my master of our discoveries now," Stone said. I snapped a few pictures before we returned to the ground floor.

By the time the dhampyr finished his call, Soames and the other hounds arrived. Leglin shook free of Soames' hold on his collar, and came to me. "*Many humans died in that room, mistress. We could smell their deaths even though the room was cleaned with,*" he paused, his eyes half-closing. "*The strong liquid you use sometimes, on white clothing.*"

"Bleach?" My goodness, the police would kill to have some elf hounds as K9 units, if the hounds could pick up scents after that kind of cleaning job.

"*Yes.*" Leglin's tail wagged double time, whacking Stone on the thigh. The dhampyr grunted and stepped out of range.

I looked at the mass of hounds. "You were amazing tonight. Thank you so much for your help. Leglin will let you know as soon as we have time for a cookout, and you'll get your steaks."

Every single one of the hounds inclined their heads and *poof!* They disappeared. I gave Leglin a super good neck scratching before planting a kiss just above his nose. "You're awesome."

Nick asked, "What now?"

"Back to the office for us. I want to add the new photos to the rest of the case stuff." Looking at Stone, I said, "Let me know if you guys have any luck undeleting the witnesses' memories."

"I will." Stone's promise was accompanied by a smile. "You've been of great assistance."

"We do our best. Talk later." I teleported the guys to Nick's truck, Leglin following on his own. Spent the drive to the office formulating questions, which could often trigger my tracking ability.

No useful threads appeared though.

Derrick had finally emailed the other photos and information sheets. After printing them out, I asked Nick to take care of printing the photos Soames and I had taken. "We'll go sort this stuff."

"Sure." He took our phones and sat down at my desk.

In the War Room, I glanced over the info sheets while Soames taped up the photos from Friday night's discovery. "I guess my 'elves as killers' idea is out."

"Unless one used an invisibility spell and a scent blocker," he replied. "I didn't catch any hint of elf where Lira was killed."

"Then they're off my list." I scanned Lira's mini-bio, and caught something. "She had a sister."

"Lira?"

"Yeah. We should see about contacting her. Maybe Lira told her something useful. Be right back." I left to find a legal pad and pen. Returning, I took a seat and began making notes. Soames finished his task just before Nick joined us. My boyfriend was frowning as he held up the stack of prints. "Where do you want these?"

"Go ahead and tape them under their owners."

He put our phones on the table and went to work. Soames dropped into a chair and pointed at my notes. "You don't think the case is over?"

"I'm not sure whoever killed Esme and her family is the same person who took out the other three. Or that the witnesses' memories were altered." Even if they had been, catching Lira's killer didn't mean he or she would confess to killing the others. I doodled question marks under the last of my notes. "Wonder what Derrick's going to do about all those bodies."

"Hide them again. I would," Nick said while coming to sit at the table. "Huge PR disaster otherwise."

"If he does, I'll find them again and tell Damian where they are. Their families deserve to know what happened to them." The men exchanged a look. "What?"

"Do that, and the media gets wind of it—which will happen because Mayor Wells is a media whore—and humans will go on the war path."

"You have a point." It wouldn't exactly be fair to paint a big, red target on the vampires who weren't running around eating people.

Good night, had I really just thought that?

"When humans do that, they tend to lump us all together," Nick added.

"Oh." Okay, I'd have to come up with a different idea. What, I didn't know, but somehow, families would learn what had happened to their loved ones. "I'll figure something out if Derrick tries to pull a cover up."

"Or you could just stay out of it."

I stared at Nick. "Excuse me?"

"You poke your nose into things you really shouldn't, Cordi. Do you honestly think someone's not already making plans to take you out before you start blabbing about finding those bodies?"

Crap, had I put him and Soames in danger, playing my hunch? "Take me out?"

"Yes, you. They know we won't say a word, because most humans are just waiting for an excuse to turn on all of us." Nick's glare scalded me. "Maybe you'll get lucky again if you keep your mouth shut."

It took a moment to find my voice after that, since I was staring at him with my mouth open. "You're just now thinking to tell me this? You couldn't do it before we paraded through the Barrows with a pack of hounds?"

He jerked back, throwing up his hands. "And put the idea in Stone's head myself? You aggravate the hell out of me a lot of the time, but I don't want you dead. Besides, you don't listen to me anyway."

Crap, it was going to turn into one of those arguments. "I do sometimes."

"No, you don't. You do what you think needs to be done, or what you think is the right thing to do, and never think about the consequences."

Soames eased his chair back and stood. "Think I'll call for a ride. See you tomorrow." He grabbed his phone and vacated, leaving the door open behind him.

Too bad I couldn't follow suit. "Look...."

"No, you look. I keep trying to tell you how things work in our world and," Nick thumped the table for each word as he finished. "You just won't listen."

"Your world? Last I checked, this is everyone's world, which means it's my world too. I got along in it before we met." Before he could respond, I said, "And not just because of luck, Nick. Do you realize you're insulting me every time you say that? That you're basically telling me I don't have any skills or knowledge at all?"

"You don't have enough knowledge."

I pushed away from the table, anger warming my chest. "I've had enough of this crap. I can't be in a relationship with someone who treats me as though I'm an idiot."

His face went slack. "What?"

"You heard me. And if that wasn't bad enough, there's your dad with all his plans and rules." Whoops. I closed my mouth, not having meant to throw that in.

Nick leaned back. "You're breaking up with me?"

"Yes."

He blinked. "Because of my dad?"

Gah. "No, but he didn't help matters any."

Nick's eyes narrowed. "You're doing it because of Logan, aren't you?"

"What the hell? This doesn't have anything to do with him."

"No?" He pointed at my phone. "You called him Sunday."

My jaw dropped. "You went through my phone?"

Nick didn't deny it. "You said you'd be busy helping your mom."

"I can't believe you went through my phone." Breaking up with him was so very much the right thing to do.

"You were with him Sunday, weren't you?"

"No. Well," I hissed and pointed at him. "He and Terra helped us Sunday. Terra's been cooped up, needed a change of scenery. Mom and Tonya were there too, and I have no idea why I'm explaining myself to you. I can spend time with my friends if I want to. I don't need your permission or approval to do it."

Nick jumped to his feet, sending his chair over backward. "You didn't even mention it."

"Because you freak the hell out," I shot back. "Just like you're doing right now. You're jealous of him for no damn reason."

"No reason? He shows up out of the blue, and the two of you are best friends immediately. You blow off any worries I have about him, and you keep secret any time you spend with him. Those are damn good reasons to be suspicious." Nick's chest was heaving. His face was flushed and his eyes had turned dark gold. When he clenched his jaws, his face kind of rippled, as though something wanted out.

He looked close to completely losing it. I tried for a calm, reasonable tone. "I told you I don't cheat. If I wanted to date Logan or anyone else, I'd break up with you first."

"You are breaking up with me," he growled.

"Not because I want to date anyone else. We don't have the same goals, and you don't trust me. You don't think I can take care of myself. That's why I'm breaking up with you." Was it my imagination, or was his skin turning kind of gray? I reached out with my empathic ability, only to recoil at the seething rage that filled him.

Okay, that was not good. "We both need to cool off a little."

"I'm fine," he ground out. "Considering the woman I love is dumping me."

"You don't look fine. You look like you're going to wolf out any second."

He closed his eyes and breathed deeply. His skin had changed, because I could see it returning to its normal tan. I took a step back, and Nick spoke without opening his eyes. "I'm not going to shift, Cordi."

"Okay." But I was going to stay out of reach in case he was wrong.

His eyes were still gold when he opened them. "I scared you. I'm sorry."

No, he hadn't. Worried me a bit yes, but it wasn't worth pointing out. "I'm sorry I've hurt you. I never meant to."

"We don't have to break up."

Oh yeah, we did, especially after this. "I care about you, Nick, but we're not going to work out. There's too many things we don't agree on."

His lips tightened. "There's compromises we could make."

I hadn't had this much trouble breaking up with a guy before, and really, really wanted to be done. "I doubt either of us will budge on some important things."

"So you get to decide we're over and it doesn't matter what I think?"

For the love of little fishies. I took a breath and blew it out. "I get to decide for me."

"But you're deciding for me too."

"Yeah, and I'm pretty sure you're going to be a lot better off without me around, pissing you off all the time." I felt like screaming. "It's late, and I need to get home."

"I'll drive you. I want to talk some more."

I shook my head. "No, I have my car."

"Come on, Cordi."

"Nick, for God's sake, back off. We're done here, okay? I'm not your girlfriend anymore. I don't want to keep explaining why, and I'm going home now. Good-bye." I stepped forward, snatched up my purse and phone, and teleported out to the parking lot. While digging for my keys, I called Leglin, who'd been napping in my office.

"Everything okay?"

I whirled around, nearly falling over my hound, to see Soames standing by the rear of my car. "Holy crap, dude. Don't sneak up on me."

"Sorry."

Leglin licked my hand. I opened the door so that he could climb in. "Your ride's not here yet?"

Soames hitched one shoulder upward, glancing toward the street. "I, ah, haven't called. Wanted to make sure things were okay before I left."

"Oh. Could you hear us?" I hoped not.

"No, but I would've heard someone breaking things. You know, if you tossed Nick into a wall or something."

Or if Nick had done something and I had screamed. I appreciated that he hadn't said that. "Thanks. Get in, and we'll drive you home."

He looked at the building. "Is he okay?"

"Mad, but breathing."

"All right."

As we pulled away, I spotted Nick leaving the office. Head down, he slowly crossed to his truck.

I felt really bad at that point, watching him, but knew I'd made the right choice.

Eleven

At the first stoplight, Soames cleared his throat. "Should I stay quiet, or is it okay to talk?"

"A distraction would be nice."

"What he said back there, about us keeping our mouths shut? That's not entirely true. I mean, I won't volunteer the information to anyone. Not right now, but when the case is over," he shrugged. "Unless Lord Whitehaven specifically tells me to keep quiet, I won't. I'll tell my Queen and Logan."

"Why them? Why not the police?"

"We're clan. What each of us does affects us all. Something like that will explode—Nick's right about it spilling over to everyone who isn't human. I can't make the decision to put the clan into jeopardy over it."

I nodded, understanding even if it frustrated me. "It's not right to leave them hidden."

"No," he agreed. "And I'm almost certain Terra and Logan will decide I should tell someone, or back you when you do. It's the right thing to do, and besides, Logan's mother disappeared. They never found her body."

"Oh." I tried to imagine my mom disappearing and never finding her. The idea squeezed my heart and brought tears to my eyes. "That's horrible."

"Maybe I shouldn't have told you about it, but I want you to know we'll probably have your back over those poor people." Soames fidgeted, picking at a non-existent thread on his jeans. "Things are better than they were, right after the Melding, but we've learned our lessons on how dangerous humans are when they're scared and angry."

"Yeah." In some places, supes had been rounded up and placed in "camps" under military guard. Santo Trueno hadn't been one of those places, and those camps hadn't lasted for long. The elves had had a lot to do with calming things down and working out solutions. But people from both groups had still died, before supes were granted full citizenship in most countries.

"Is it hard, living in the Palisades?"

Soames chuckled. "It sucks in oh, so many ways, but we were

outcasts, just like most of the humans who live there. They've mostly accepted us."

Not exactly what I expected to hear, after years of news reports detailing how awful and violent that area was. Then again, they were shifters and could take care of themselves. At least as long as a big, organized group didn't go after them, intending to wipe them out. "Well, that's good."

I arrived home a few minutes after four AM, and dropped into bed as soon as possible. It felt as though my eyes had barely closed when my fairy godfather, Sal, decided to pay a visit.

The darkness became a lush, tropical garden. I could feel the warmth of the sun, and a hint of coolness as a breeze rustled leaves around me.

Peaceful place, until a voice spoke from behind me. "What is it with you, child? Do you truly enjoy flinging yourself headlong into danger?"

Turning, I studied him. Sal looked like a short, elderly Native American man, his face a mass of deep wrinkles, and his long hair a silvery white. His dark eyes were clear, and I knew he had a set of strong, white chompers hidden behind his thin lips.

"Well?"

"I like your outfit." He wore buckskins, plain except for fringing down the side of each leg, and a touch of beadwork at the neck of the long-sleeved tunic. The beadwork didn't look Native American to me, not that I was an expert or anything.

"Thank you, but a compliment isn't an answer to my question."

"I like doing my job and solving cases."

"Commendable."

"You sound like Mr. Whitehaven."

Sal ignored that. "Once again, you're in grave danger."

"Duh. I know where the vampires hid the bodies."

He rolled his eyes. "Not that, but yes, you are in immediate danger from vampires. You really should choose your enemies more carefully."

I snorted. "Right."

"However, you are improving in the area of choosing friends."

Was he talking about Nick? My eyes narrowed. How did he know so damn much about what went on in my life? "Are you a god?"

"Took you long enough to figure that out."

My turn to ignore something. Yippee. "Which god are you?"

Sal chuckled. "For me to know, and you to find out."

Hm, maybe Loki, the Trickster? I really needed to find out more about gods in general. Logan had told me that gods considered people investments of sorts. "Is there something you want me to do?"

"Absolutely. I want you to survive. No, not just survive, but to thrive." He grinned, showing off his pearly whites.

"Color me suspicious of a god who says that's all he wants. The other two I've met weren't exactly nice guys. One treated me like an interesting bug he'd found, and the other tried to eat me."

"Yes, well, the years haven't been kind to Apep. He's gone a bit," Sal twirled his forefinger beside his head. "And Cernunnos isn't a bad fellow, but he does lack a decent bedside manner." He leaned forward to whisper, "He hangs out with animals more than people, you know."

"Uh huh. But you, you're friendly and only concerned with my well-being. Right." I crossed my arms and stared at him.

"Of course. You're one of the cool kids, handed a bushel of powerful toys to play with. I'm interested in what you'll do with those toys."

"I've already decided: I use my abilities to help people."

Sal cocked his head, an impish grin playing about his lips as he squinted at me. "Ah, but is that what you'll always do? The world's a steaming cesspool, and living in it affects everyone differently. In a manner of speaking, it refines them down to their basic components."

He was getting too deep for me. "And?"

"In ten years, assuming you live that long, will you still be little Miss Helpful, concerned for others? How about in twenty years?" Sal moved closer, his dark gaze intent and his grin gone. "When you have years of witnessing the evil people are capable of, the pettiness that can drive them, their glorious depravity, will you still feel a desire to play this small part? To continue helping people?"

I let my arms fall. "Going Dark Side isn't on my agenda, if that's what you're asking. The world does suck a lot, but there's good people in it. I want to be one of them."

Sal stepped back, his lips pursed. "I'm eager to see what happens with you, Discordia. You're an interesting little girl."

"Gee, thanks."

He laughed. "Try to stay alive, child."

"Now that is on my agenda. Right up at number one."

"Good." He faded away, the garden going with him.

My eyes opened. "Freakin' gods."

I stumbled into the kitchen around noon to make coffee, only to discover Mom had set up the coffeemaker for me. She'd also left a plate of blackberry muffins, with a note that they were my breakfast, and she'd taken Red to work with her.

Dogs gathered around as I leaned against the counter, pulling the plastic wrap off the plate. "I'm not awake enough to share."

"We really like muffins," Bone said, watching while I pulled the paper baking cup off the first muffin.

"There's only six."

"You're going to hog them all?"

I looked down. "You guys had breakfast. You're all going to get fat if we keep giving you treats."

"We're dogs, genius. We don't care about being fat." Diablo jumped up, resting his paws on the edge of the counter, and eyed the plate. *"That many is six?"*

"With this one." I took a bite, wishing the coffee would hurry up and finish brewing. "Red really likes my mom, huh?"

"We all do. You know, the little ones go crazy stupid when they get sweet stuff. It's pretty funny." Bone let his tongue loll out when an indignant chorus rose. Squishy felt particularly miffed, and began chewing on one of Bone's front legs.

"Hey, no biting." I bent to pull her away, and Diablo stole one of my muffins. "Dude!"

"Mm." He licked his lips, muffin gone, paper and all.

"Crap." Now I had to let everyone have a bite to be fair. By the time I'd parceled the treats out, there were only two muffins left. "Thanks a lot, Diablo."

The black pit bull grinned, still licking his chops. I pushed the plate away from the countertop's edge before pouring myself a cup of coffee. "By the way, Nick won't be coming over anymore. We broke up last night."

Diablo was the first to respond, with a grunted *"Good."*

His opinion reflected the general doggy consensus, leaving me rather huffy. Even dogs wanted to weigh in on my damn choices. "Thanks a lot, guys. This has been an awesome start to my day."

Dread over seeing Nick again so soon after breaking up caused me to drag my feet. I didn't reach the office until after three, only to see his truck wasn't in the parking lot.

Tabitha greeted me with a bright smile and "Mr. Whitehaven wants to see you in his office."

She wore a black headband with fuzzy, fake tiger ears and a black and white sweater set over a black skirt, with orange and black striped socks to complete the ensemble. I needed to step up my game. Mr. Whitehaven wouldn't be out of place on the cover of a men's fashion magazine, while Kate, and now Tabitha, could be poster girls for cool. Me, I was in well-worn jeans, black running shoes, and plain, dark blue sweatshirt. I looked like a couch potato. "Okay, thanks. Cute ears."

Wondering if Nick had called in sick, and silently berating myself for the relief I felt that he wasn't there, I dropped off my purse in my office before going to see the boss. "Hi. What's up?"

He looked up from the file he was reading. "Good afternoon, Discordia. Please, have a seat."

"Sure." I dropped onto the couch while he set the file aside.

"Nicholas was in early this morning, and requested a leave of absence."

"Oh." Well, more guilt for me. Perfect addition to my day. "I kind of broke up with him last night."

"I see. I granted his request, though that does leave us short-handed on your current case."

And that was why office romances were a bad idea. "We can manage. There may not be much case left to work on." I filled him in on the events of last night, including finding all the bodies and discovering that Stone was a dhampyr, and Derrick's son. "I think Soames and I can handle the rest okay, with Leglin and Stone, if Derrick leaves him on loan to us."

"If you're certain?" When I nodded, he glanced at the file. "It sounds as though the case is going well."

"Pretty well. Um, Nick said some vampire might decide to keep me from talking, you know, about finding those bodies. Like, permanently."

Mr. Whitehaven smiled. "I wouldn't worry overmuch on that score. Most will realize that you'd inform me of your findings. Removing you wouldn't solve their problem."

Well, duh. Why hadn't we thought of that? "That's a relief."

"I did say 'most'. Don't allow your guard to drop."

"Right." I picked at the hem of my sweatshirt. "What do you think Derrick will do about them?"

"Whatever he can that will generate good will and press for his people."

How would that even be possible? "Can't wait to see how he manages that."

"I'm rather interested, myself."

We traded a smile, and I stood. "Guess I'd better get to work."

"Very well. Have a good evening."

"You too." I left for the War Room, and once there, realized I wanted someone to bounce ideas off of. Someone with more experience as a detective.

Fortunately, I knew just who to call.

Twelve

While waiting for Damian to arrive, I called Soames to see if he was ready, and teleported to bring him to the office rather than fight traffic.

Once we'd arrived, Soames asked, "What are we doing today?"

"Haven't heard from our client about the witnesses yet. I've called Damian. Have you met him?"

"Sort of. He's the police detective who did that time-lapse spell, right?"

I nodded. "I want to run what we know so far by him, plus some ideas about what our next steps should be. But let's not mention last night's big discovery, okay?"

"The bodies, yeah. Okay. I'll get the photos down." Soames did that while I went to fetch us some drinks from the break room. He'd finished by time I returned, the photos tucked into the case folder we were keeping on hand. "Why do you want a second opinion?"

I waved at the table and as we sat down, hid the case folder under my purse. "Because I'm not relying on my psychic abilities for this case. Can't, since they're not exactly being helpful. We're having to do this old school, and I don't have loads of experience solving cases that way."

"Huh." He sat back, glancing at the white boards. "Could've fooled me. Not that I know a lot about it, but I think you've made pretty good progress."

A warm glow of pleasure enveloped me. "That's 'we', dude. We're a team."

He smiled. "Okay, we've made pretty good progress."

"Damian has a few years of experience on us, and I trust him to point out stuff we may not think of."

"All right, makes sense. So what are your ideas about our next steps?"

I shrugged, wanting to see what sort of ideas he'd toss out first, and if any of them would line up with my ideas. "You tell me. Pretend you've just come into the case. What pops up?"

Soames propped his arm on the table and rubbed his chin. "Uh...what about trying to find more connections between the murder victims? We know three weren't really on board the Don't

Kill Humans train. But Esme and family were, so how do they fit in with those three? Or do they at all? Are we looking for one killer, or two?"

"Good." He was coming up with the same questions. "Any other ideas?"

Brow furrowing, he thought about it for a minute before shaking his head. "None that I can think of right now."

"Cool. I'm guessing we're probably on the right track, because you have the same questions I do." We heard Tabitha greeting someone, and when she received a response, I said, "Damian's here."

After I'd introduced the two men, I spread my arms out. "Ta-dah. Our case wall. How'd we do?"

Damian walked down to look over the first section. "Why are there so many vics here?"

"All members of the same family."

He nodded and looked over the other sections. "No related vics with these?"

"None that we currently know about." It wasn't an actual lie, considering the context of his question.

Damian stared at Merriven's photo. "Isn't this the vamp who turned your friend?"

"Yup."

"Did you celebrate his demise?"

I laughed. "Haven't had time to yet."

"Case keeping you that busy?" He stepped backward until his rear made contact with the table, leaned against it, and crossed his arms.

"Yeah."

"Where's Nick?"

I winced. "Leave of absence. We broke up."

"Ah. Was it the arguing?"

"Got it in one." Close enough anyway.

Damian nodded. "I completely understand." He freed one arm to wave his hand toward the line of boards. "Well, this looks good. Now tell me how the vics are connected."

"Lady Esme, Lords Holmesby, Merriven, and Tanaka were all council members."

"What about her family?"

Soames glanced at me before responding. "Ramon was Esme's heir apparent to her council seat. He was a master too, but the other four weren't."

"All right. What's the theory for why they were killed?"

My turn. "Politics. There's two political parties, one that wants to

stick to the old ways—killing when they feed—and the other doesn't."
I paused for breath. "They were all members of the second party."

"Uh huh." Damian re-crossed his arms. "Correct me if I'm wrong,
but when you spoke to me about Ginger's situation, didn't you
mention she'd claimed Merriven was draining some of his blood
donors?"

"Yes." A hint of bitterness tainted my voice. "Not that anyone
bothered to check it out."

"Don't be so quick to judge, Cordi. I did check, quietly, and the
only person who made that claim against him was your friend."
Damian offered me a faint smile. "We can't do full-scale
investigations based on the claim of a single, unhappy vampire
fledgling."

That drove me to defend her. "She wasn't lying."

"Why do you believe her?"

"She never lied to me."

Damian tucked his chin, focusing his sky-blue gaze on me. "Being
a vampire wasn't what she expected. She was abused and desperate.
People in such situations have been known to mix lies with truth in
order to convince others to help them."

My anger rose. "Not her. Ginger wouldn't do that."

"How can you be so certain?"

Because she was my friend. I opened my mouth, intending to tell
him that, and something slunk out of the back of my mind. Out from
where I shoved all the nightmare-inducing things I'd seen.

I didn't really want to look at it, but it was waving around in
response to Damian's question. Closing my eyes, I focused on it.

"Cordi?"

"Give me a minute. I'm remembering some...oh." I shuddered and
fought to put the memory back where it'd come from. It wasn't mine.
The memory didn't want to return to the darkness, fighting my
attempts to push it away, throwing blood across my mind between
flashes of the terrified faces of two strangers. I knew the room they
were dying in. Soames had taken pictures of it. And I learned
something else too, before finally winning.

Opening my eyes, my heart racing and gasping for air, I focused
on Damian. "I believe her because I saw her memory of one of
Merriven's 'dinner parties'." I pointed at the white boards. "That's
why I thought those two looked familiar when I first saw their
photos. They were there."

Damian dropped his arms. "Why didn't you tell me this before?"

"It was almost two years ago." I hadn't turned twenty-one yet, was
still a scared kid trying to keep my abilities under control. "It scared
me."

He relaxed. "You buried it."

"Yeah."

"All right, let's move on, unless you need a minute?"

"No, I'm good." I fought the urge to tuck my trembling hands behind my back. The vamps hadn't just eaten dinner. They'd played with their food first. "But that means those three all shared a secret. That's how they're connected."

"Right." Damian regarded the boards again. "Are you certain Esme's family didn't have the same secret?"

"Yes, because of the gargoyles."

His head snapped around so he could see me, and Damian winced, lifting his hand to rub his neck. "Gargoyles?"

Soames jumped in to explain those, and Damian's eyes bulged when he reached the part about Tase using me as a hiding place. "Wait. It touched you?"

"Yeah, he was pretty scared. It's why I didn't try questioning him, even though he has to be a witness."

My warlock friend sputtered, his face flushing dark pink. "A witness? Is that all...good night, Cordi. Don't you know what it means when a gargoyle...of course you don't. Let's put it this way: I know a coven of witches who'd sacrifice their own body parts to attract a gargoyle."

Wow. "Okay, why?"

"Why, she asks." Damian lifted his gaze to the ceiling. "My God."

"Psychic here, not a witch," I reminded him, feeling miffed. "It's not like I've crossed paths with gargoyles before."

"Right." He glanced at his watch. "I have to get back soon. Go by the shop when you can, and ask David to tell you about gargoyles."

"Okay. Where were we?"

Soames answered. "I think we're stuck on how Esme's family could be connected to the other three victims."

"Right." I nibbled my thumbnail. "First thought that comes to mind is that Esme discovered their secret. She was killed first."

That received an approving nod from Damian. "Do you have any potential leads to work that angle?"

"Lira had a sister. We were thinking of finding her, see if she knows anything."

"Good plan. How about any psychic leads?"

"Nope. My abilities may as well be on vacation."

"Aw." He grinned. "You're having to play this old school."

"Yep, and it kind of sucks. But it's fun too. I mean, having to put everything together like it's a giant puzzle with a thousand pieces. Not the dead people part."

"Wait until you solve it. You'll feel high for days." He checked his watch again. "I have to go."

"Thanks for helping. I owe you a lunch."

"Out, or will you cook?"

I laughed. "Your choice."

"You're cooking then. Good luck." He shook Soames's hand, gave me a peck on the cheek, and left.

Grinning, I rubbed my hands together. "Let's find Lira's sister."

Angelique Herrera proved relatively easy to locate, thanks to an online directory. She didn't answer when I called, and I didn't leave a message. "It's not even seven yet, so let's drop by and see if we can catch her at home."

"Sure. Dinner after that?" Soames asked.

"Yes, I'm starving. Had to share my breakfast with the dogs." Everyone else had left for the day, including Mr. Whitehaven. I locked up behind us when we left.

David Bowie's "Under Pressure" poured from my car's speakers when I started it, and Soames instantly began singing along. He had a nice voice.

Angelique's apartment complex was near the community college. I drove the maze of parking lots until Soames spotted her apartment number. "That one, right there."

There wasn't an empty spot to borrow for parking. I drove out and around, parking on the street behind her building. The sun had sunk below the horizon by then, leaving the sky the dark blue that precedes full dark. No stars visible, obscured by too many street lights. Even with all the lighting, I shivered. "Let's go see if she's home."

After we walked around the end of her building, Soames touched my arm and murmured, "There's a vampire on the roof of the building across from hers."

I didn't look up, though I wanted to, but I did drop my mental shield a few inches. "I don't feel anything, so it can't be a master vamp."

"What do you want to do?"

"How about this?" I grabbed his arm, glanced upward, and teleported to the roof and behind the vampire. The vampire rose from his crouch, peering over the roof's edge, as I let go of Soames.

The shifter wasted no time leaping into action, taking one long step to grab the vampire's arm, whirl it around, and take a swing. I winced at the crack of fist on jaw, but cheered when the vamp dropped. "Woohoo. Nice punch, dude."

"Thanks. Don't suppose you have handcuffs?"

"Nope." I removed my thin, faux leather belt. "Will this work?"

"Let's find out." Soames took the belt, and flipped the vamp face down. Roughly five seconds later, he'd pulled the vamp's arms back and wound my belt around his victim's wrists before buckling it tight. He rolled our prisoner back over, and hefted him up onto a shoulder. Soames stood up in a smooth movement, not a sign of strain on his face. "Can I get a ride down?"

"What, you can't jump?" I grinned to make certain he knew I was teasing, and walked over to take hold of his elbow. "Going down."

Soames looked at me when we appeared in front of Angelique's apartment door. "Really?"

"He was watching her, not us. Let's see if we can find out why." I knocked. Soames listened, nodding when he heard someone on the other side.

"Who is it?"

"Angelique Herrera? My name's Discord Jones, and I'm a private investigator. We're here about your sister, Lira."

"She's dead."

Well, at least I wouldn't have to break that news to her. "I know, and you have our sympathies. May we speak to you for a few minutes?"

"Do you have a badge?"

"No, ma'am. I can show you my PI license though. Just a minute." I hurriedly dug out my wallet, and opened it to display my license. Holding it up to the peephole, I said, "Here it is."

Silence, followed by the sliding of a dead bolt and Angelique opening the door a crack. Just enough for me to see part of her face, including one dark brown eye, and the chain still in place. "Let me see it again."

"Sure." I moved to give her a good look of my license. "My associate here is Soames, and the lump on his shoulder is a vampire we caught watching your place."

Her eye widened. "You caught a vampire?"

I smiled. "He's a shifter, and I'm a psychic. Poor little vamp was outclassed tonight."

She swallowed hard enough that I heard it. "Why do you want to talk to me?"

"We're investigating your sister's murder."

Her one-eyed gaze flicked from me to Soames before she moved out of sight and pushed the door closed. The chain scraped as she removed it, and she opened the door wide, stepping back. "Come in."

"Thank you." She was tiny, four-one or -two, and no bigger around than a toothpick. Her slender neck bore a lot of round, white scars, and looked too fragile to support the weight of her thick, black ponytail, much less the dozen or so necklaces she wore. Angelique was barefoot, dressed in black leggings and an oversized, rose pink, cowl necked sweater.

In two steps, I was clear of the entryway and entering her living room. Soames followed me, dumping the vamp on a floral-patterned couch. I scanned the room while Angelique relocked the door. It was spotless and comfortably furnished, but the mini-blinds had a slat out of place right about eye level for our hostess to have been watching out the front window. Soames noticed that too, but didn't say anything. He leaned against the wall by the couch, hooking his thumbs in his belt loops.

I sat down on one of the chairs that matched the couch. Angelique took the other one, pulling her feet up and wrapping her arms around her bent knees. "What do you want to know?"

Straight to the point. "Did your sister have any enemies that you know about?"

She shrugged. "She was a vampire."

"And you were a blood donor."

One of her hands crept up to touch her neck, calling my attention to a set of jagged scars. They looked as though a vamp had bitten down and then jerked away without fully opening its mouth. She frowned. "So?"

"As a blood donor, you must've spent a lot of time in the Barrows."

"Yeah."

My mind was scrambling. "Lira wasn't turned all that long ago. Your scars are old." None had the pink appearance of freshly healed wounds. "You stopped donating before she was turned?"

Angelique's eyes slid away from my face. "Yeah."

"May I ask why?"

Her fingertips brushed across the jagged scars. "I was attacked. Had a vamp that didn't want to stop drinking."

Oh, we were getting somewhere now, and I even thought I might know where. "How did you get away?"

"Another vamp came along, and spooked him, I guess. He let go and took off." She shivered, probably thinking of how near a miss she'd had. "Just disappeared."

"Do you know who the other vamp was?" I held my breath, waiting for her to answer, and remembering Tase's mumbling: *Invisible, invisible, invisible.*

"His name was Ramon."

Hello, Giant Freaking Clue. "Lady Esme's Ramon?"

"Yeah. That's how Lira met her. They called her to come get me." Angelique blinked. I had the impression she'd surprised herself by volunteering the information.

"Okay." Puzzle pieces were raining down, and falling into place. "Any idea why that guy was watching your place?"

Her face tightened, and she shrugged, plucking at the hem of her sweater. Darn it. I looked over at Soames, who freed a hand and flicked his finger across his throat. With a tilt of my head toward her, I silently invited him to speak.

He cleared his throat. "Miss Herrera, you're wearing a lot of silver. Interesting thing about silver: It's like poison to vamps."

My new thing learned for the day. Useful now and in the future, so an excellent thing to learn. "You're afraid because there's a vamp after you. Who?"

She touched the necklaces, the scars, and dropped her arm to hug her knees to her chest. "It's the one who attacked me. They were trying to find him. Said he was breaking the law, trying to drain me."

I nodded, hoping my expression looked properly encouraging.

"Lira said, last time we talked, they'd tracked down three they thought were killing people. She was sure one of them was him."

Three. Holy crap. I pulled the folder out of my purse and collected the photos of the three dead vampire lords. "Please look at these."

Her hand trembled as she took the photos. The second photo captured her full attention. "Him. He's the one that nearly killed me."

I took the photos back and checked. "Merriven."

Angelique licked her lips. "I think he killed them."

I shook my head. "Maybe Esme and Lira, but he was killed before the others were."

She stared at me. "No."

"No, what? They found his ashes in his home."

"He can't be dead, because I saw him three nights ago. That's why," she gestured at her cascade of silver necklaces. "I haven't left here since I saw him. He wants me dead too."

She was afraid, could've thought she saw him. I wasn't willing to take that chance. "Well, we're not going to let that happen. Go pack a bag and put some shoes on. I'm going to take you somewhere safe."

I left Soames standing guard over the unconscious vampire, and teleported Angelique to the Blue Orb. More specifically, David's kitchen on the second floor. He jumped, the knife he was spreading mayo with clattering to the floor. "I really wish you'd call ahead."

"Sorry. I need a favor."

"Okay, what?" He bent to retrieve the butter knife.

I explained, while Angelique studied him, doubt all over her face. David grinned, an edge of fierceness sharpening it. "Absolutely, she can stay here."

"He's a warlock, and he won't let a vamp near you."

Angelique looked from him to me. "You're sure?"

Admittedly, David didn't look like a magical bad ass, in his beige slacks and baggy blue cardigan over a white button down shirt. The glasses holding on for dear life at the tip of his nose certainly didn't help. "This is his Clark Kent. If a vamp shows up, you'll get to see him turn into Superman."

David blushed bright pink.

"I have a question too. How difficult are invisibility spells?"

"Ingredients aren't difficult to find, but to find a spell that actually works? Nearly impossible," David said.

"Thanks." I patted Angelique's shoulder, smiled at them both, and teleported.

Soames was flexing his right hand. "He came to."

"Oh." The vamp was out cold. Again. I shrugged. "Angelique's safe."

Soames didn't ask where I'd taken her, just hauled the vampire up to sling the limp body over his shoulder. I touched the shifter's arm, teleporting us out to my car. We dumped the vamp into the hatchback area and climbed in. I sighed. "Looks like we're about done with this case, depending on what this guy has to tell us."

"Are we going to question him?"

I shook my head. "Nope. We're going to drop by the office for a minute. I need to check something before we call Derrick to set up a meeting. He can have Sleepy."

Soames grinned. "Then let's go."

Thirteen

The stop by the office was as brief as I'd promised Soames. I only needed to refresh my memory about something, and grab a few of the scene photos, before meeting with Derrick.

Back in my car, I called Stone. "Hey, we've found some new info we want to share. May I teleport directly to the library?"

"Yes, that will be fine. We had less than satisfactory results with the witnesses."

"Bummer. We'll be there in fifteen minutes." I pushed the button on my car stereo to end the call. "I'm really liking this hands free thing."

Soames was frowning. "I'm guessing that means they didn't have their memories altered. But how could he make himself invisible?"

"I have a theory about that, and it doesn't include spells. David says that invisibility spells that really work are nearly impossible to come up with."

"What's your theory?"

"You'll just have to wait. No sense in repeating myself. By the way, nice job mentioning the silver thing."

He looked at me. "You really didn't know that?"

"Nope."

"Huh." His gaze went back to our passenger. "Well, you can set vamps on fire with a thought, so I guess no one felt you needed a different way to deal with them."

"Guess not." I knew there were big gaps in my knowledge of the supernatural, but sometimes, there were gaps I didn't even realize existed. "Will silver kill them?"

"A silver knife or bullet to the heart should work just like a stake. Other than that, it'll burn them, and weaken them as long as there's particles of silver in their systems. Oh, and they can't break silver chains."

More useful knowledge. "I thought silver was bad for shifters."

Soames chuckled. "No. Enough damage can overload our ability to heal. Burning us works, so does beheading. Of course, beheading works on most things. But silver itself isn't a problem for us."

"Wow."

He looked at me. "What?"

"I'm having an 'Oh my God, my life is completely off the rails' moment. I have a vampire in my cargo area, and we're discussing ways to kill people."

"You should've been on our side of the Sundering. This was daily conversation for us."

How freaking sad was that? I changed the subject, since we were near an entrance to the Barrows. "Oh, look. A parking space."

Our prisoner regained consciousness once more before we pulled him out of my car, but I kept Soames from clocking him a third time. "Awake is kind of necessary for questioning."

"Right." Soames settled for a tight grip on the vamp's arm, just above the elbow. "Ready."

Derrick and Stone were waiting in the library when we appeared. I smiled before making myself comfy on the couch, across from Derrick. "We come bearing gifts."

"I see. Who is this?" Derrick studied our prisoner, who looked pretty scruffy now that I could see him conscious and bright-eyed with what appeared to be fear.

"No clue. I'll get to him in a minute." I was ready to enjoy myself. "First, the reason the witnesses' memories weren't altered is because the killer was invisible. Ever hear of telekinetic invisibility?"

Derrick shook his head.

"Okay, but you do know that kinetic abilities are basically about manipulating matter. A psychic with telekinesis can," I concentrated, lifting the coffee table a few inches. "Make things move or," I put the table down. "Hold up your hands like you're going to push something."

Derrick complied. I concentrated, thickening the air between us. "Okay, push."

His hands moved an inch before encountering resistance. Surprise flashed across his face.

"Technically, that's aerokinesis, but I try to keep things simple for the sake of my sanity." Everyone but the prisoner chuckled, though I'm not sure what they thought was funny. "Light is also matter, so someone with kinetic abilities could learn to manipulate light too. And if you bend light around anything the right way, it becomes invisible."

Derrick realized he still had his hands up, and dropped them. "The killer has this ability."

"That's what I'm thinking, yeah. I checked with an expert, and invisibility spells aren't easy to successfully create. He didn't teleport, or there'd be dead witnesses or they would've had their memories altered." I retrieved the photos I'd collected. "Look at these. The first one is from the scene where Merriven's ashes were found." I'd scanned the photos quickly, and grabbed the first one I saw that had a blur in it that I didn't take. "And this one, I took at Esme's of Deborah's ashes."

"The blurs?" Stone asked, leaning over Derrick's shoulder for a better look.

"Yep. Notice how they're both tall, say about person height?"

"Yes." Derrick passed both photos to Stone. "So, telekinetic invisibility."

Time to drop the big bomb. "I know who your killer is too. Merriven."

Derrick's lips twisted. "Miss Jones...."

"You found ashes at his place, but that doesn't mean they were his ashes. Plus, I have a witness who saw him after he was supposedly killed, and possibly his motive for faking his own death."

My satisfaction knew no bounds when Derrick and Stone both came to full attention. I told them everything we'd learned from Angelique first. "Top that with this: I thought Tanaka and Holmesby looked familiar the first time I saw their photos. Didn't know why, since I couldn't remember meeting either of them. Earlier today, my memory was triggered, and I recalled something I'd picked up from Ginger." My smile had faded. "It was one of Merriven's 'dinner parties', where they were draining humans. Holmesby and Tanaka were there."

"It's rather convenient you remembered such a thing tonight," Stone said, handing the photos back to Derrick.

"When I was first turned, one of the most difficult changes were the memories transferred to me. It's quite easy to convince yourself to forget some things, in order to preserve your sanity." Derrick met my gaze, and I nodded.

"Anyway, I think Esme found evidence the other three were killing people. Merriven killed her and Lira, and maybe the attention that drew made Holmesby and Tanaka rethink being involved with Merriven. Or maybe Merriven decided a clean sweep was best." I stopped to take a breath. "But there's one final loose end: Angelique. She's safe, and I bet he," I pointed at the scruffy vamp. "Can probably help you find Merriven."

Scruffy wilted when Derrick and Stone focused on him. "I was hired to take the woman, not kill her. I don't know who wanted her."

Whether he did or not, it really wasn't my problem anymore. I felt certain we'd solved the case, and it was up to Derrick to find Merriven. "Betting you guys can take it from here."

"Indeed. Escort the prisoner downstairs," Derrick ordered. Stone complied, shutting the library doors behind them. The vampire lord gestured for Soames to join me on the couch. "We do have another matter to discuss."

"The bodies."

"Yes." He stared at us for a moment. "It would be highly detrimental to our efforts to reveal them *en masse.*"

No freaking kidding. "Yes, I understand that."

"However, because we are determined to build a working relationship with humanity, I can assure you that those poor unfortunates will find their ways home." Derrick leaned forward, focusing on me. "We simply need time to formulate the least devastating method of revealing their existence."

"You want me to keep my mouth shut for now. I did tell Mr. Whitehaven about them."

Derrick sat back. "I expected no less. May I ask his response?"

"He said you'd probably tell people, once you figured out a way to do it so that it made your people look good."

"Lord Whitehaven is wise."

"So yeah, I'll stay quiet. For now."

Derrick smiled. "Thank you, Miss Jones, and you as well, Mr. Soames."

The sun was rising as I drove home from the Palisades after dropping off Soames. We'd eaten dinner before returning to the office, and I'd walked him through writing and filing the case report.

It felt really good to have worked the case through mostly using plain old investigation methods. I felt like a real detective for the first time since joining Arcane Solutions.

When I pulled into the driveway at Mom's, Tonya was coming down the block from the direction of the park. Leglin, Kyra, Bone, and Diablo clustered around her, all of their tails up and wagging. She preferred to take the pit bulls out when other people weren't likely to be around. Less chance of anyone freaking out over their appearance that way.

I waited so that we entered the house together. It was completely silent. "Was Mom not up when you left?"

"She was in the shower."

"Weird, the Chihuahuas should be, hey!" All of the big dogs took off for the kitchen, bumping us hard enough that we both staggered to keep our balance. "Guess they're hungry. Mom?"

No answer from her, but a deep, mournful howl rose. I met Tonya's wide eyes and shivered before rushing to the kitchen. She was a half-step behind me as I shoved the swinging door open. "Oh my God."

"What?" Tonya scooted to one side, peeking over my shoulder. "Oh no. Sunny!"

She tried to push past me, but I stopped her. "Go. Call 911."

"But...."

"Call 911," I repeated, staring at Leglin. My hound stood at the end of the island in the middle of the kitchen, his huge paws inches from a pool of blood. "Now."

Tonya retreated. The rest of the big dogs were clumped together behind Leglin, all staring at whomever lay behind the center island. I didn't notice the Chihuahuas huddled under the kitchen table behind them, not at first. The pool of blood, and the blood splashed all over the cabinets had me transfixed. My gaze rose, following a slash of wet crimson upward. There was even blood on the ceiling.

I took a deep breath and walked into the kitchen, letting the door swing shut behind me. Another one before stepping around the center island to see where the blood had come from.

Red lay on his side, his throat and stomach ripped open. His open eyes stared at nothing, and his mouth was half-opened. Three severed fingers lay right in front of his muzzle, half-submerged in blood. They weren't Mom's fingers.

She was nowhere to be seen. I noticed two smeared lines of blood beginning at the edge of the pool and extending to the back door. The handle was broken and the door open a few inches.

That kicked me into motion. I rushed to the door, throwing it open, and out onto the back patio. "Mom!"

No answer. Closing my eyes, I mentally shouted for her over and over again, but to no avail.

Nothing to hear, not until a siren began wailing a few blocks away.

"It was vampires. Two of them."

The cop questioning me blinked. "And you know that how?"

"My dogs can smell them, and the smaller ones were here. They saw what happened." Speck shivered and whimpered, curled into a tiny ball in my lap. I covered him with my hand, feeling numb. My voice sounded far away every time I spoke. So did everyone else's. "There were two vampires."

"Uh huh. Do you, ah, talk to your dogs often?"

I looked up, having been staring at Red's body. Tonya was in the living room, being questioned by another cop. "Yes, actually, I do."

"I see." His expression made it clear he thought I'd lost my mind.

"I'm a psychic, not a nutcase, Officer," I checked his name tag. "Rothman. Being able to communicate with dogs is one of the perks." Not strictly true, but whatever. "Call Detective Herde or Schumacher, or hell, for that matter, call Chief Stannett. Any one of them can vouch for me. I've helped you guys out several times."

"Oh." His face brightened. "You're that Jones."

"Yeah." I saw a familiar face enter the kitchen, but couldn't dredge up the paramedic's name. "Are they taking Red?"

"Yes, ma'am. Coroner will need to look him over."

"I want him back." I'd find somewhere nice to bury him. He deserved it. The evidence of how hard he'd tried to save Mom was splattered everywhere. "Tell them that."

"I will." Rothman stepped away to speak to the paramedics. My head hurt, and my eyes felt hot and swollen though I hadn't cried yet. My chest ached, and my hands were cold. I stroked Speck's shivering body.

"Discord."

"What?" The familiar-looking paramedic was standing in front of me. "You kept touching the damn arrow."

"Yep, that's me, the Toucher of Arrows. Name's Mike." He smiled, his cornflower blue eyes scanning my face. "I'm going to check you over, okay?"

"I'm fine."

"Right. How about we pretend I'm the expert and let me decide whether you are?"

"Whatever." I let him do his thing. "Is Tonya all right?"

"Understandably freaked the hell out, but not hysterical." Mike checked my eyes. "I'm sorry about your dog."

"So am I." His partner had finished bagging Red's body. I licked my lips, which felt dry and hot. "Did Rothman tell you I want him back?"

"Yes, and I will personally let the coroner know you will be in to claim him. When's the last time you ate? Slept?" Once I'd answered his questions, he patted my shoulder. "You need to eat something and get some sleep. Don't make me come back here because you collapsed from exhaustion."

My stare made him shake his head. "I mean it, Missy. You won't help your mother if you don't keep yourself in good running order."

"Yeah." I blinked, the fog beginning to lift from my brain. I needed to make a phone call. Two phone calls, one of which I wasn't looking forward to making at all.

Dad needed to know what had happened.

"It's not your fault," was the first thing Dad said once I'd stopped babbling. "Do you need me to come over? I can be there in fifteen."

"No. I need to get everyone out of here so I can do something about finding her." I scrubbed my hand over my wet cheeks.

"All right. I love you, Cordi, and I have faith you'll find her. Call me for anything. Tell me if I can do anything. Okay?"

Yeah, right. Like I was going to stick him in the middle of this mess when Mom was already missing and one of the dogs was dead. "Okay, Dad. Love you. Bye."

"Keep me posted. I mean that. Bye."

Ending the call, I opened the bathroom door to check my room for cops. No one had come in.

Good, because I didn't want them overhearing the next call.

Fourteen

Stone's phone rang four times before he answered in a sleep-graveled voice. "Hello?"

"Listen up, you son of a blood-sucking bitch. You tell Derrick I want my mother back," I snarled. "Alive and unharmed. We said we'd keep quiet. There wasn't any reason to..."

"Miss Jones?"

"...to take her and kill my dog."

"What?" He sounded more awake.

"You heard me. I want her back now, or I'm coming and I'm going to start burning the Barrows to the ground when I get there."

"I don't know what you're talking about," he said. "Tell me what's happened."

"Two vampires broke into my house this morning." My voice broke. "They killed one of my dogs and took my mother."

"You have my deepest sympathies, but I swear we know nothing about it, Miss Jones. My mas...father believes you to be a woman of honor. He believes you'll keep your word."

Which meant Derrick had no reason to kidnap Mom. But if he hadn't taken her, who had?

"Miss Jones, are you there?"

"Yes."

"You're certain it was vampires?"

"Yes." Oh God, what was happening to Mom right now? What if she was...I cut that thought off.

"Can you bring me a photo of her?" Stone asked.

"Why?"

He responded in a patient tone. "We'll need a photo so we know who we're searching for."

Oh. "I can bring one."

"The quicker, the better. I'll gather some men. We can begin searching immediately."

A single tear escaped. I hadn't expected help from him or Derrick. "I'll be there in a few minutes."

"Meet me in the library," he said before ending the call.

I left my bathroom at a fast walk, and ran directly into Officer Rothman. "Sorry, can't talk now."

He followed me when I brushed past, right into the living room. Tonya sat on the couch, her red-rimmed eyes following me as I crossed to grab a photo of Mom and me off the mantel. Her arms were locked around her husky's neck.

"Miss Jones." Rothman tapped me on the shoulder.

"I have to take this to the Barrows."

"Wait a minute."

"No. There's a vampire lord who's going to help me look for her. They know the Barrows best, and can find her faster than you can." I looked at Tonya. "Pack a bag. Take all the dogs with you to David's, and tell him what happened. He'll call Kate in. Stay there until I tell you it's safe to come home."

She nodded. "All right."

"And call me if they come up with anything useful."

"I will."

I turned my attention back to Rothman. "Do not leave her here alone."

"Miss Jones, you can't leave right now."

"Yeah? Watch me." I teleported.

Stone was in the library when I arrived. He took the photo and waved his hand at the table. "There's coffee. Help yourself. I'll be back in a few minutes."

Once he vacated the room, I called for Leglin. My hound silently appeared, his mournful eyes rising to meet mine. "I want you to go back and keep an eye on Tonya until she leaves. After she pulls out of the driveway, come back to me."

"*Yes, mistress.*" He disappeared, and my knees began shaking. I had to sit down. Somehow I'd left my purse and phone home. I really needed my phone.

Once before, I'd teleported an object without being in contact with it: Damian's gun. Theoretically, I should be able to do it again. Except for the whole bit about I hadn't exactly been aware of what I was doing the first time, what with being under a curse and all.

Yet I really, really needed my phone.

I closed my eyes, envisioning the device and willing it to appear so hard, my head throbbed in protest. After a minute or two, a small weight dropped into my lap. I opened my eyes and felt a smile start at the sight of my phone. It felt wrong to be smiling. Grabbing my phone to begin scrolling through the contact list, I quickly found the number I wanted and made the call.

"Hello, Miss Jones. To what do I owe the pleasure of this call?" Thorandryll, elf prince, asked after the third ring. I wondered if he knew I'd borrowed some of his hounds while answering.

"I need help. My mom's been kidnapped by vampires."

"I'm truly sorry to hear that. Unfortunately, I'm in Canada at the moment, taking care of some rather delicate business matters."

"That's okay, I just need to borrow your hounds. All of them."

"Do you have permission from a council member to take them into the Barrows?"

Crap, really? I should've just jacked them like I did the first time, instead of calling to ask the favor. "Not exactly. I mean, not yet."

"I'll contact Alleryn...do you have his number? No?" he gave me his healer's number. "Once you've been granted permission, call him. He'll order the hounds to obey you and send them to you."

"Okay, thanks."

"We'll discuss the price later."

My blood pressure soared. "Are you seriously going to charge me something because my mother's missing? You know what? Never freakin' mind."

Before I could end the call, Thorandryll said, "Wait. No fee for the use of my pack, Miss Jones. My apologies."

"Thank you, and apology accepted."

Stone returned as I ended the call. "I'm having copies of the photo made, and have three dozen of our people ready to begin searching."

"That's not enough." I wasn't certain exactly how large the Barrows were, but thirty-six people, even vampires, surely couldn't cover the whole area very quickly.

"My master sleeps, as do many others of our house. I can't leave the estate unprotected." Stone scrubbed a hand over his face, drawing the stubble on his cheeks and chin to my attention. "We have others out searching for Merriven, so we're a little short-handed right now."

Perfect opportunity to bring up the call I'd just made. "Prince Thorandryll has agreed to loan me his hounds. I just need permission from a council member first."

The dhampyr grimaced. "Lord Derrick would probably give permission, but he won't awaken for another two hours."

"Can't you give it, in his place?" Time was speeding by. How long had it been since Mom was dragged out of the house? I checked the time on my phone. At least over four hours. The less time it took to find Mom, the better for her.

Stone's grimace became a full-fledged frown. "No, I can't speak for him on this. I know he'd want to instigate a search, but whether he'd definitely agree to having a large pack of elven hounds running loose...I simply can't. I'm sorry."

Part of me wanted to tell him to stuff it, I was calling in the hounds anyway. Kind of shabby since he'd offered to help, and was helping. I forced my anger away. It wasn't going to help find Mom. "Okay, we'll wait until he wakes up. What can you do now?"

"Send people to search the homes of those under watch, and to check certain areas where illegal activities regularly take place."

Solid plan. Cover the places an unwilling donor might be hidden away. Made sense, but... "What do you mean by 'those under watch'?"

Stone poured two cups of coffee, the heavenly aroma of dark roast spilling into the air. "Think of drug addicts. They have difficulty kicking the habit. There are vampires addicted to the rush of feeling that occurs when experiencing the life of their victims slipping away. Those who admit their addiction and ask for help are given it."

Bloodaholics Anonymous, the twelve-step program for death-addicted vamps. The idea tickled my funny bone even under the circumstances, and laughter bubbled out of me. It leeched away my tension and anger, leaving only my fear for Mom. My laughter became sobs, and I buried my face in my hands, aware of the dhampyr leaving the room.

Stone returned to slide a box of tissues onto my lap while sitting down beside me. The mighty—that would be me—fell low about two seconds after he tentatively put his arm around my shoulders. He was warm, not cold. Felt human.

I turned to bury my face in his shoulder to finish my crying session, and felt the beating of his heart against my cheek. Another reminder that he wasn't a vampire. My sobs became hiccups, and after the third one jolted through me, I straightened to swipe a fistful of tissues from the box.

While I dried my face and made a huge production of blowing my nose, Stone rose to return to the other sofa. Not looking up, I muttered, "Thanks."

"You're welcome," he said. "We already have teams out scouring the Barrows for Merriven. I'll see that they receive copies of your mother's photo."

Right back to business. I liked that, and nodded. "I'll walk around, do some telepathic scanning for her."

"Once your backup arrives."

"I knew I forgot something."

Stone took a drink of his coffee, his lips twisting slightly. It had cooled off during my mini-breakdown. "Since we don't know who took your mother, or why, I don't think it's a good idea for you to wander around unaccompanied."

Neither did I. "My hound will be here soon."

"More backup than him. Elf hounds are quite intelligent, but they're still dogs. They can be tricked or overwhelmed."

Maybe, and being kidnapped myself certainly wouldn't help Mom. I sighed, picking up my phone, which had fallen between the sofa cushions. "Let me make some calls."

"I'll be there soon," Kate said before hanging up. "Make certain there's a map."

"I will." She'd promised to tell the boss what was going on.

My next call was to Jo, because Leglin had appeared. He climbed onto the sofa with me, my purse dangling by its strap from his mouth. "Thanks, bub."

I took it and scooted to give him room to lie down. Leglin pinned me with one of his forelegs and his head across my thighs. Jo finally answered. "Cordi, what the hell is going on? Tonya showed up, her car full of dogs, and all we understood was 'Sunny' and 'vampires'."

Reminded that I wasn't the only one dependent upon Mom being okay, I asked, "Is she okay?"

"David's house guest is making her tea and trying to calm her down. Now what was she trying to tell us?"

My explanation didn't take long. Jo offered to come, but I pointed out the same thing Stone had: We didn't really know what was going on, who had Mom, or why. "Kate's on her way and I have Leglin with me." I stroked my hound's back, or at least as far down it as I could reach. "Tonya and Angelique need to be kept safe. Some of Derrick's people are already out searching for Mom."

"Okay, is Nick with you?"

"We broke up. He's not working right now."

Jo snorted. "Call him. He likes Sunny. He'll help look for her."

"Yeah." I had no intention of doing it. Didn't need the additional drama.

"Call if you need anything."

"I will, thanks." Ending that call, I wasn't sure who to call next. Ronnie was out of town, and Damian would find out through work, if he hadn't already. The tigers had Terra to worry about. Of course, Soames was on loan. I decided to call him.

"Hey, something came up. Can you meet me at Derrick's?"

"Sure." He sounded groggy. I'd woken him. "But it'll take me a half hour or so."

"That's fine. See you when you get here." It'd probably take him longer than that, but there wasn't much I could do about it. Time wasn't an energy I knew how to manipulate. If I did, I'd have already done it to go back in time, to be at the house before the vampires arrived. Mom and Red would be safe, because I would've been there to save them.

Fifteen

About twenty hours later, in spite of vampires, telepathic scanning, and elf hounds, we'd learned nothing new and hadn't found my mother. I saw the sun rising for the second time since I'd last slept as Mr. Whitehaven escorted me out of the Barrows Thursday morning. "Threatening those who are assisting you isn't conducive to keeping them properly motivated."

"Sorry," I mumbled, my last adrenalin surge wearing off. Exhausted, sick with fear, and angry at the lack of success—at any progress whatsoever—I only vaguely remembered what all I'd said while having a screaming meltdown.

"Dane will take you home to rest. Don't return here until nightfall," my boss ordered. "I will stay, and immediately inform you of anything important."

"But," I couldn't come up with a coherent protest and closed my mouth. Didn't resist as they bundled me into Soames's truck. In fact, I fell asleep before Soames pulled the vehicle away from the curb.

When I woke, it was with no idea where I was or what time it was. The room was dark and my eyes felt dry and crusty. Rolling over, I managed to make out enough to realize it was Logan's bedroom. What the hell was I doing here?

The low murmur of voices in the living room caught my attention, but so did an insistent message from my bladder. First things first.

A few minutes later, I opened the door to find Terra sitting on the couch, her eyes glued to a daytime soap opera. "That stuff will rot your brain."

"Discord." The blonde teen jumped to her feet and nearly knocked me off mine as she threw her arms around me. "You're awake. Are you hungry? You didn't wake up at all when Soames carried you in this morning. We thought you'd gotten hurt, but then he explained everything. Logan said to put you to bed and let you sleep."

"Oh, thanks." She'd said "this morning", so I hadn't slept more than the day away. I saw my purse and phone on the kitchen table. "Has anyone called? Is Logan downstairs?"

Terra moved back and gave me a critical look. "You still look tired. No calls yet, and no, Logan's not downstairs. I can make coffee if you want?"

"Please." I sat down at the kitchen table while she hurried to start some coffee. My head ached, so I dropped it into my hands, elbows resting on the table. I flat didn't know what to do. Call and nag the searchers? Really helpful, Cordi. "Where is Logan?"

"He took most of the clan and went to help look for Sunny," Terra said, carefully measuring out coffee.

Which left her less guarded than she should be, with Mega Douche out and about. I didn't know whether to be upset or pleased that Logan would do that for my mom. "Do you have any ibuprofen or aspirin?"

"No, but I'll send someone to pick some up." Terra finished setting up the coffeemaker, hit the brew button, and went to crack open the front door. "Teague, Discord needs some ibuprofen."

"All right," I heard the lion shifter reply. She shut the door and turned around, only to stand there looking at me.

"Um, anything else I can do?"

Come up with a location for my mom? Kate hadn't had any luck at that. I leaned back and managed a smile. "No, but thanks."

Terra returned the smile. "Okay, coffee will be ready soon. I think Tansy's about your size, so you can take a shower while I grab some clean clothes for you."

Over forty-eight hours in the same clothes. Right. I pulled up the neck of my shirt for a sniff and winced. "That would be totally awesome."

Showered and freshly clothed, I left Terra's bathroom. She'd been busy: toast, coffee, and the requested painkiller waited for me on the kitchen table. Her anxious smile sent me straight to the table to sit down. "Thank you."

"I didn't burn anything this time."

"It looks great." I leaned to sniff the wonderful coffee perfume while opening the bottle of ibuprofen. Ten minutes later, I'd polished off a second cup and four pieces of toast. My phone rang, and my buttery fingertips smeared the screen as I grabbed and answered it. "Hello?"

"You're up, good," Logan said. "I have good and bad news. We found out where Merriven was holed up, and now we know he has Sunny, because we found a few of her hairs there."

Tears welled at the information, and I couldn't stop them from escaping. My voice shook. "Okay."

"We're trying to track them. Kate's still working with the map."

I swallowed hard, gazing across the table at Terra's worried face.

"I'll be there soon."

"Do me a favor first. Take Terra and Teague somewhere safe. Have her tell the others to come with you. Okay?"

"Are you sure?"

"Yes. I trust your judgment on where safe is."

"Okay." I hoped David wouldn't mind another pair of surprise guests. The Blue Orb was the safest place I knew of, with Jo and him, plus their familiars, there. Broad daylight and a steady flow of foot traffic in the area didn't hurt. "I really appreciate this."

"This is what friends do. See you soon." He ended the call.

I passed on his plan to Terra, who nodded and went to the front door. "I need everyone on the first floor in five minutes, and they need to be ready to leave."

"Why?" Teague didn't like the idea of moving once she explained. "I know this building."

"I'll make sure you're given a tour," I called out, stuffing my phone in my purse. Terra shut the door before he could protest more.

She went to her room, returning in a few seconds with a backpack. "Logan taught me to be prepared."

"Good deal." After I slung my purse strap over my head and shoved an arm through it, we left the apartment.

Down the stairs we went, and I slowed as we made the last turn on the stairwell to find six people waiting. Terra took charge. "You're all going with Discord to meet Logan and help find her mother."

A tall, black-haired woman with high cheekbones and thin lips stepped to the front of the small group. "And leave you with only the lion as guard?"

"No. Discord's going to take us somewhere safe first."

The woman frowned, sharpening the angles of her face even more, and focused her pale brown eyes on me. "So you're the psychic the Protector is willing to risk our Queen for."

Before I could respond, Terra spoke. "This is Danielle, and those two are her cousins, Ted and Rob. You know Alanna and Soames, and the last is Gabriel."

"Hi." Danielle's cousins were also tall. Ted was built on rangy lines, but Rob was a solid, barrel-chested slab of meat from the neck down.

Alanna decided to jump in. "Danielle, are you saying the three of you aren't capable of guarding our Queen?"

The other woman looked down her nose at the petite brunette. "If there were a concentrated attack here, with so few of us?"

"Enough." Terra's frosty tone drew everyone's attention to her. "Don't question Logan's decisions. Discord is in charge until you meet up with Logan. Alanna, assist her. Is everyone clear?"

Even I nodded, impressed by the note of command in her voice. Not that I didn't feel some sympathy for Danielle's point. Logan really shouldn't have left Terra with only seven people. Of course, I wasn't the boss of him.

"Good." Terra looked at me. "We're ready when you are."

"Now is good." I held out my hands to her and Teague. As soon as they both gripped mine, I teleported us to David's kitchen.

Tonya, Jo, and Angelique jumped or squeaked as we appeared. Jo recovered first, tucking strands of her dark auburn hair behind her ear. "More guests. We're going to run out of room, Cordi."

"Sorry. I promised Logan I'd bring them somewhere safe, and this is it."

She grinned. "That it is. You should see some of the surprises David's come up with. I pity the vamp who tries breaking in here."

"Any news?" Tonya's shoulders slumped when I shook my head.

"None except they found out that Merriven has my mom."

Angelique shivered, hugging herself. "I'm so sorry."

"She's not dead." I hoped. He'd taken her for a reason, and the only ones I could think of all pointed toward revenge against me. I'd killed his fledgling, and revealed his continued existence to Derrick, and through him, the rest of the vampire council. He had to have taken Mom to use her as a bargaining chip. Of course, that didn't mean he hadn't hurt her, but I shoved that thought away. "We'll find her. I gotta go. Later."

I teleported back to the clan's apartment building. Danielle was scowling, Alanna smiling, and the four men were looking everywhere but at either of them. Not having time to find out what was going on, I just held my hands out. "We're teleporting."

Once everyone joined hands, that's exactly what we did.

We appeared just before the steps up to Derrick's front door. Not exactly where I'd intended to arrive, but it worked. Wondering if my teleportation ability was wonky because of stress, I checked things out. The antique-attired footmen weren't on duty. Instead, two vamps dressed in jeans, dark button-up shirts, and black sports coats were. I hadn't seen them before, but to my surprise, that didn't turn out to be a problem.

"Miss Jones, welcome. Our master is in the library with others, and is expecting you." While the one on the right spoke, the other opened the front doors.

"Thank you." We trooped inside, instantly having to dodge vampires rushing about, and walked down to the library. The doors were open so we could hear voices inside.

Derrick, Kate, Logan, and a few others were gathered on and around the sofas and coffee table, looking at a map.

"What's going on?" My question turned heads. Logan left the group to greet us, or maybe just me, because he put his arm around my shoulders before pressing his cheek to mine.

"We're marking out new search areas to assign. How are you holding up?"

"Okay."

He took me at my word. "Good. Come have a seat, we'll fill you in."

I didn't really have a choice, since he started walking with his arm still around me. Once I'd dropped onto the sofa next to Kate, Logan perched on the armrest next to me. Those who'd come with me found places to stand, and I noticed Danielle, flanked by her cousins, glaring at me over Derrick's head. Her problem with me would just have to wait.

"We've now searched roughly half of the Barrows." Derrick pointed at the map, indicating the area someone had shaded with a pencil. "We currently have teams searching here."

They were working a strip straight across the map, right along the edge of the shaded section. "Teams consist of four, with one of my more telepathically talented people included in each. They're scanning, as well as mentally shouting your mother's name and listening for a response."

I leaned forward, nodding, and he continued. "This is where we discovered Merriven had been hiding. It's an empty manse."

"Stone and I personally covered every inch of the place," Logan said, patting my back.

It occurred to me that I hadn't exactly been grateful for all the help Derrick and his dhampyr son were extending. Saying "Thank you" didn't seem like enough, especially after my meltdown that morning. But it was all I could do right then. I met Derrick's eyes. "I really appreciate all that you're doing. I know my mom will too."

All the vampire did was smile and say, "Family is one of the most important benefits one can have."

Logan cleared his throat, and Derrick's smile faded as the vampire glanced at him. "We're covering ground pretty quickly. By tomorrow evening, we'll have searched the entire Barrows."

I took a breath. What if we didn't find them? That was the million-dollar question. If they weren't in the Barrows, where did we begin looking next? Letting the breath out, I decided to focus on one thing at a time. "I'll go out with a team."

Kate opened her hand to reveal her locator crystal. "I'll keep trying with this."

"You haven't had any luck at all?" When she solemnly shook her head, I bit my lip. "Where's Percy and my hound?"

I didn't say Leglin's name, in case he was in the middle of something. Kate closed her fingers around the crystal. "They're out searching too. Mr. Whitehaven is on one of the teams as well."

To her, I didn't say "thank you". I leaned enough to kiss her on the cheek. She swatted my knee, her lips curving ever so briefly. "Go on, Jones, and make yourself useful."

Sixteen

My arrival with six more volunteers necessitated some reorganization. We left the library to Kate, joining the vampire hustle going on in the main hall. I leaned against a wall between a painting and a suit of armor, closing my eyes. All the concentration I had went toward one question: Where was my mom?

Which of my more passive abilities responded didn't truly matter, as long as one did with a good clue. My tracking ability would be best, but beggars couldn't be choosers, and I was definitely begging.

To absolutely no avail, and gradually, the sensation of being stared at opened my eyes.

Logan smiled, but the way his attention was instantly on Derrick and their conversation made it unlikely he'd been staring. Probably had just glanced my way. I turned my head, scanning the crowd, and found the source of the staring. Danielle stood thirty or so feet away, her eyebrows pinched together over the bridge of her nose, and her lips turned down at their corners.

Minor annoyance. I closed my eyes again, focused, and then with every bit of power I could gather, telepathically shouted "*Mom!*"

The main hall filled with the hissing of a hundred snakes. Startled, I opened my eyes to find I'd become a magnet for vampiric eyeballs. "Um, whoops?"

Derrick laughed. "Quite impressive, Miss Jones, but may I suggest you save your energy for now?"

My face burning, I nodded. "Yeah, sorry."

Just what I'd always wanted: To make a complete ass out of myself in front of a few dozen vampires. I moved away from the wall and turned so that I faced the painting. My blush faded while I pretended to study it, but impatience began to build. How long did it take to work seven more people into the roster?

It didn't help that Danielle continued staring at me. She went from minor annoyance to major aggravation in less than five minutes. Counting to ten didn't help, but it did keep me from stomping over to poke her in the eye and give her something else to think about.

When I couldn't take her narrowed-eye glaring anymore, I walked over to Alanna and asked in a whisper, "What's her problem?"

"Two things, well, I guess really three. One, she's not senior queen. Terra decided it should be time as a clan member and not age that decided seniority. Danielle doesn't like having to bow down to women younger than her, and she really doesn't like the fact I'm senior queen." Alanna's blue eyes sparkled. "Two, her status is important to her, and I'm certain she has her eye on Logan, since he's the highest ranked guy, at least until Terra chooses her Consort. But he doesn't treat her any differently than he does everyone else. And three, you're not clan but we're helping you."

"Oh." More than I had expected to learn.

She touched my arm. "Ignore her. You have more important things to worry about. But I will give her this: She follows orders and does her part. She'll be thorough, search every nook and cranny of each area she's assigned to search."

That was good to hear, because I could deal with Danielle's dislike, deserved or not, as long as she didn't use it as an excuse to shirk from looking for Mom.

Logan and Derrick finally called everyone to order to assign new search areas, and tell us who would be part of which team.

I tried not to frown when told I'd be on Logan's team, along with Danielle.

At least it didn't take long to get moving after that.

We searched for three hours, and found nothing. Frustration and worry combined to make for a toxic emotional brew, one threatening to boil over constantly. I wanted to start burning things until someone admitted to seeing Mom or Merriven.

"Time for a break," Logan said as we exited the last shop on the last block of our assigned area and headed for the four-seater utility vehicle we'd been given for wheels. The vampire who owned the shop sneered out an "I told you so" none of us acknowledged.

Plopping into the front passenger seat, I braced my foot on the abbreviated dash and crossed my arms. "This is getting us exactly nowhere."

Logan turned the key, his tone mild. "We're narrowing down the possibilities of where she's being held."

"It's been over thirty-six hours." The more time that passed, the less chance of finding Mom. Alive, anyway. Anger at myself for thinking that flared and hardened my voice. "He could've done anything to her. Be doing anything to her."

"Correct," Danielle said from the back. "After this much time, she's probably dead or turned."

I twisted around to glare at her. She'd been making snide remarks the entire time we'd searched. "Hey, Miss Sunshine. How about you drink a big old cup of Shut the Hell Up?"

She bared her teeth. "Don't give me orders, human."

"Both of you had better cool it, or I'll pull this vehicle over," Logan snapped. I turned around and re-crossed my arms.

"Terra's right. You do sound like a parent."

He glanced at me. "Was that an insult?"

"No. Maybe." I dropped one arm and raised the other to rake my fingers through my hair. "I'm sorry. This is driving me crazy. It's like my worst nightmare ever."

"A loved one being kidnapped is probably most people's nightmare."

"Yeah, but I bet it's not most people's fault when it happens to their mother or whoever."

Logan shot me a look. "It's not your fault. Merriven chose to do this."

My laugh tasted bitter. "Yeah well, I doubt he just accidentally sent two goons to my mom's house to kill Red and drag her off to God knows where."

Danielle decided to throw in her two cents again. "If you feel this is your fault, perhaps you should reconsider involving yourself in other people's business. Especially if those other people are supes."

"Uh, hello? That's pretty much the job description for a PI: Get involved in other people's business. They hire me to get involved in their business."

"And just look how well that's working out for you now."

"You're not helping, Danielle," Logan said.

"No, she's not. Can I teleport her into a wall?"

He aimed a frown at me. "No."

"I would like to see you try."

I snorted. "I'd like to see you try and stop me from doing it."

She hissed, and Logan hit the brakes. My chest collided with my knee. "Ow, what the hell?"

"I've listened to you snipe at each other for three hours straight, and I've had enough." The low, silky soft timbre of his voice sent a chill down my spine, and brought the fine hairs on the back of my neck to quivering attention. "I know you're scared for Sunny, but that's not a free pass to take it out on Danielle or anyone else."

I closed my mouth and nodded, only then remembering what Soames had told me about Logan's mother disappearing. This had to be dredging up a lot of bad stuff for Logan, and I felt awful for not remembering earlier. No wonder he'd been so quick to volunteer the clan.

Logan turned to look at Danielle. "Whether you approve or not, Discord is both an ally and friend of our clan. Extend the courtesy that deserves."

She nodded, and it was nice to see her eyes were as wide as mine felt. His jaw clenched, lips a straight slash, Logan stared at her. Then at me. "Apologizing to each other would be a good move right now."

"Do we have to kiss before making up?" When his eyebrows lowered, I sighed. "I'm sorry for being a jerk to you, Danielle. Thank you for helping look for my mother."

"I apologize for being difficult during this trying time. And you're welcome."

Her apology wasn't targeted at me, but Logan didn't seem to realize it and I wasn't going to make a fuss about it with him glaring at us. Instead, I smiled at him. "We're good now."

He didn't smile back, but his voice returned to normal. "Thank you."

As he put the little vehicle back into motion, I made a note to myself: Don't aggravate Logan. He actually does have a temper.

A well-controlled one, but he'd sounded pretty freaking scary for a minute there. I didn't want to be the one to make him lose his temper. Or even be around if he did. I glanced at him, the image of an atomic explosion appearing in my mind.

Yep, something like that.

After experiencing the tiny taste of Logan's temper, I opted to spend the next few hours trying to kick my abilities into gear.

I sat in Derrick's library with Kate, who'd replaced the silver chain her locator crystal normally hung from with a few strands of my mom's hair that Logan had found earlier. Another strand was wound around my forefinger, and I rubbed it with my thumb, eyes closed and concentrating. The only result was a growing headache. A huff of air opened my eyes to find Kate staring at her unmoving crystal. She growled. "What is it with this not working?"

"At least I'm not the only one it's happening to. I'm getting jack. No flashes, no threads, no visions, nothing."

Kate dropped the crystal to the tabletop and rubbed her temples. "Are we absolutely certain demons don't have her? The last time this happened was with Zoe."

"Logan told me vampires are demonic, but I've never had trouble with my abilities when dealing with them before." I hissed in frustration, carefully unwinding Mom's hair and returning it to the waiting baggie. "I feel like a huge failure."

"We do have nearly two hundred people out, canvassing the Barrows." Kate scowled down at the map. "I can't believe one vampire is this good at hiding."

"He has that invisibility thing going for him, and this is the Barrows: Pocket Realm Mishmash."

My witchy friend kicked off her amethyst-colored high heels and wiggled her toes before standing. She moved away from the sofas and table to begin pacing, strumming her fingers on her thigh. "If I can't get a location, that may mean he has her in an unmapped area."

"Which does us no good."

Kate spun around, her pale fuchsia painted lips—Did her lipstick ever wear off like normal people's?—forming a perfect O. "Tell me, Jones, have you attempted psychometry on anything belonging to Merriven?"

"No." I shuddered, knowing where she was going with it.

"Don't you think you should?"

"Yes, as soon as I can get something belonging to him." I glanced at the closed doors. Derrick was busy managing everything. It could be a while before he was able to send someone over to Merriven's estate. "Put your shoes back on. We're going to take a quick trip."

Kate slammed the last drawer shut. "No underwear."

"What?"

"He doesn't own underwear. A commando vampire."

"Ugh, I so didn't need to know that. Thanks bunches." I went back to picking through the wooden valet on top of the dresser. The pen I used tick-tapped against cufflinks, rings, and what I thought might be cloak pins. "Um, why were you looking for his underwear?"

"You need something he's worn a lot."

No one to blame but me. I'd had to ask the question. "That's so gross, Kate. I don't want a porno vision."

She sniffed, half-turning and putting her hands on her hips to survey the rest of the room. "I suppose that means we'll skip taking the sheets?"

"You're making me queasy."

"Hmph." Kate walked over the big, four-poster bed. "I'll check the night stand."

"I'm afraid of what you'll find." Or not find, and decide to remark on. While she spilled the contents of the stand's small drawer onto the bed, I selected a particular ring, relying on the memory from Ginger. A large, square-cut emerald flashed from the wide gold band. The stone had looked darker when he had his hand wrapped around a woman's neck. Dropping it into a baggie, I shivered. "I found something I can use."

"Me, too. He kept a diary." Kate twirled, holding up a small, leather-bound journal with a brass lock. "Couldn't find the key."

"Like I need one." Not that I had any intention of opening the journal. Didn't need to read Merriven's private thoughts to know he was a sadistic scumbag. Touching it would probably be bad enough. "That'll work. Let's get back."

Back at the library, Derrick stood staring down at the map with a frown on his face. The vampire lord noted our appearance with a flick of his eyes. "Where have you two been?"

"Gathering goodies." Kate brandished the journal. "We looted Count No Pants' resting place."

"Would you please not mention that particular bit of info anymore? Like, ever again?" I asked, retrieving my phone to check the time. Almost midnight.

Derrick rubbed the tip of his nose, possibly to hide a smile. "You went to Merriven's estate?"

"Yeah. I haven't tried psychometry on anything of his." Trading my phone for the bagged ring, I held it up to show him. "Now I will."

"Your associate, Mr. Soames, mentioned a rather peculiar reaction you had to Ramon's ring. I have to ask if it's safe for you to handle that one."

I shrugged. "Kate's got a mean left hook, and you're a vampire. I think you're both safe if I have an attack of the biteys."

He cocked his head to study Kate. She smiled, tossing the journal onto the coffee table, a picture of punky, retro elegance in her heels, Fifties-inspired black dress, fishnet stockings, and perfect, if overly purple, makeup. "Don't judge a witch by her superb fashion sense, McFang."

Derrick suppressed a smile, the corners of his lips twitching. "Of course not. All right, Miss Jones. It appears we're ready when you are, but I do have a suggestion to make first."

"Sure." I sat down on one of the sofas.

"Before you touch the ring, imagine an open box. When the thirst strikes, force it into that box."

Useful, if I could manage to do it. "Is that what you do?"

"It's what we all do, otherwise, the thirst controls us."

I nodded and unzipped the baggie to drop the ring onto the table. "Okay, thanks."

He sat down across from me. Kate casually slipped off her heels, the better to move fast, before perching on the armrest of his sofa. I hadn't been kidding about her left hook. She was the one who had peeled me off Mr. Whitehaven the time I'd tried to bite him, and knocked me cross-eyed.

Closing my eyes, I imagined a box, but changed my mind.

Cardboard wasn't going to cut it. I imagined an iron chest with double locks instead, bigger on the inside like the famous Doctor's blue box.

Satisfied with that, I opened my eyes and scooped up the ring.

Nothing happened. I tossed the ring into my other hand. Nope. "I'm really tired of being a psychic with vaca...." My psychometry kicked in, flooding my brain with green-tinted images. "Aw, crap."

With a scowl, I dropped the ring onto the table. "It's one of those objects."

"Beg pardon?" Derrick said.

"Wants to show me its whole history in chronological order. Completely useless for quick info."

"Then try his diary." Kate leaned forward to shove the journal closer to me.

After flicking the ring aside, I picked up the little book. Blood thirst poured into me, hot and demanding, rocking my head back. "Ahh."

Derrick's eyes widened when I focused on him. "That is truly fascinating. The box, Miss Jones. Use it."

The thirst wasn't interested in him, but Kate? It forced my gaze toward her. She slipped off the armrest, her hands clenching into fists. "Jones, the crimson eyes are not a good look on you. Use the damn box before I have to ruin my manicure."

My slow blink made her shake her head and try a different approach. "You're wasting time. Your mother needs you."

"Mom." I closed my eyes, forcing some space between the thirst and myself. Recalling my little iron chest, I began fighting to divert the blood thirst into it. Took a bit of doing, but I managed it. "Okay."

"Eyes?" Kate prompted. I opened them wide to let her have a look. She settled back on the armrest. "Much better. Carry on."

"Are you receiving anything useful?" Derrick asked.

"Flashes of faces. He loves writing in it." I shivered. "Pets it after he's locked it. Ugh. Wait."

A wall of bones and stone. Dark rooms carved into rock, coffins lying inside them. "I think I have something. Are there cata..." A thin line appeared in my head, twin threads of silver and gold forming it. "Holy crap. I have a trail."

Kate squealed, clapping her hands together. I dropped the journal and lunged to my feet, pausing just long enough to snatch up my purse before taking off for the doors.

"Miss Jones!"

"She has to follow it now," Kate told him while I threw open the doors. Derrick rushed past me, calling out instructions as I ran down the main hall to the front doors.

A crowd of vampires followed, their lord and master leading them, but he caught up as I cleared the gates. "Miss Jones, wait. If it leads to the catacombs, they're nearly seven miles away."

I halted. The thread might fade before I reached its end. I couldn't run full out that far.

"I have someone diverting the teams to there. We'll take one of the vehicles."

"Okay."

He smiled, his eyes bright. "I have no idea what you're following."

A vamp pulled up in one of the little utility vehicles and hopped out. Derrick took the driver's seat, and I hurried around to the front passenger seat. "Me either, really. Drive."

The top speed of the utility vehicle was faster than I could run, but my vampire chauffeur didn't seem to have much practice driving it. He took turns at full speed, which was around forty miles per hour, never applying brakes, and I nearly fell out twice.

It was sort of fun, shouting directions at him and holding on for dear life while tourists and vampires scattered before us, his people speeding along in our wake in more of the little vehicles. Or maybe hope and relief made it fun. I finally had a lead.

Derrick nearly plowed into a trio of shifters when we arrived at the catacombs' entrance. As they leaped clear, he yanked the wheel around, turning the vehicle sharply enough that two of its wheels left the ground.

"Hit the brakes," I yelled, clinging to my seat with both hands, my feet threatening to go through the dashboard because I was bracing so hard. Derrick stomped, and we lurched to a halt, the vehicle thumping down onto all four wheels again. We both looked around, taking in the startled or scowling faces, before looking at each other and starting to laugh.

I climbed out, still laughing, to stagger toward the entrance, which was outlined by carvings of skeletons. The entrance was roughly thirty feet wide, and about the same tall at its highest point. A big archway leading to the underworld, and judging by the number of humans, also a big tourist trap.

The thread faded as I took a step through the entrance, but it didn't matter.

We knew where to look.

I stopped laughing, but still wore a smile when Derrick appeared beside me. "Let's get busy."

Seventeen

"This is the only entrance," Derrick said, while we watched his people clear the area. He'd ordered the catacombs closed.

As I'd thought, it was a tourist trap. The buildings surrounding the big square before the entrance consisted of restaurants and souvenir shops, and there were even a few hotels.

"Who in their right mind comes down here for a vacation?"

"You'd be surprised. We have families, business people, and of course, the singles looking for a temporary vampire lover so they'll have a story to tell." He was checking every face that passed by us, even though people had to pass through the line of vampires stretching out in a half-circle around the entrance. Everyone was watching for Merriven or my mother.

Ten minutes later, the last few people trickled out and the all-clear was given. No alarm had been raised. I saw Logan pull up, Danielle smiling in the front passenger seat, apparently enjoying having him all to herself.

Derrick's people and the shifters gathered together at the entrance.

"I'm going to call Alleryn, ask him to send the hounds again."

The vampire lord nodded before stepping away to explain why we were here.

"It's almost three AM, Cordi," Alleryn said when he answered.

"You sound grumpy."

He hmphed. "I presume you require the pack?"

"Yes, please, and I have Derrick's permission again."

"All right. I'll send them to Leglin shortly."

"Thank you. Sorry I woke you." Ending the call, I looked around, but didn't see my hound. "Leglin."

He appeared, his tail dragging and his head held lower than usual. I knelt to hug his neck. "Poor dude, you're exhausted."

"And I have found nothing."

"It's okay, I did. Your pack mates are on their way. After they get here, I want you to go back to Derrick's library. Kate should still be there. I'll call her so she'll get you some food. Eat it and get some sleep."

He gave a slow wag of tail. "*But we have not yet found your lady mother.*"

I hugged him again. "We will, but what if I need you later and you're too tired to help? You need to be rested. Okay?"

"*Yes, mistress.*"

"Thanks for working your tail off."

Leglin turned his head to check his hindquarters. "*My tail is attached.*"

I chuckled, scratching behind both of his ears. "It's a saying, bub."

Logan cleared the crowd, walking over to crouch down beside us. "How are you doing?"

"Better now. I'm sorry about earlier."

He nodded. "Leglin looks tired."

So did he. The skin under his eyes was beginning to darken. "When's the last time you took a break?"

"When we dropped you off."

"That was six hours ago. What time did you get to the Barrows?"

Logan shrugged. "About an hour after Soames carried you in this morning."

"Geeze, dude. Take everyone and go home. Eat and sleep."

"Already sent everyone but those who came with you home." He sighed. "Can't have them all miss work again."

I felt guilty, not having thought about people skipping work to help search. "Seriously, go on home. I really appreciate everything, but...."

"We're good."

"But...."

"We are," he insisted. "We'll help search the catacombs. Derrick's already offered food and beds at his place."

"Oh." Another thing I hadn't thought of: Where I'd go for rest, whether we found Mom or not. I didn't want to go home, to the blood-soaked kitchen and no company.

"He won't mind one more. He'll have different people here to take over before dawn." Logan patted my back. "The hounds are here."

People were fidgeting when I checked the crowd, and some stepped hurriedly aside as I watched. Enid came into view. The hound spotted us and trotted over. I smiled at her. "Hi, thanks for coming."

"*What are we to do?*"

I explained, and by the time I'd finished, Derrick had everyone headed into the catacombs.

"We've miles to cover, but my people know the catacombs," Derrick said as we climbed the roughly hewn stone steps. "We're one of the few families who still inter those lost to us here."

There were five levels, and he'd already informed us that the catacombs were a pocket realm. He'd also insisted on enlarging the search teams from four to six people. After a little discussion, I'd split the pack into five groups, one for each level. There were eighteen to twenty hounds in each group. They'd just stared at me when I asked them to not split into smaller groups of less than three or five while searching.

We didn't know how many minions Merriven had. All of his people had left his estate after his faked demise. I didn't want to lose any of the hounds because one ran into more vamps than it could handle alone.

Not only for their sakes. There was a little selfishness involved in my decision. Thorandryll would probably decide I owed him if any of his hounds were killed.

"I didn't know these were here," I said.

"You've never come to our actual entertainment district." Derrick glanced over his shoulder at me. "Your clients hire you to retrieve their badly behaving sons, daughters, wives, and husbands. Family members who've usually managed to attach themselves to someone of importance."

He had a point. Few of our clients lacked money, though I knew for a fact that Mr. Whitehaven would reduce rates for those who really needed our services.

The stairs weren't very wide, and there wasn't a guard rail to keep anyone from falling over their edge. We were in single file, Derrick in the lead. Logan was behind me, Danielle behind him. Enid and three other hounds followed her, and bringing up the rear were two of Derrick's minions.

We weren't the only ones heading for the upper level. The catacombs' "cathedral" was a long, narrow cavern, and stairs had been hacked into the stone on both sides at each end.

The plan was simple: Start at the ends and meet in the middle. Replacements would arrive at some point for the vamps who pulled the sunrise deady-bye shift.

My legs were growing heavy. "Haven't you heard of elevators yet?"

"Little metal boxes that carry people from floor to floor? Why yes, I have. They'd ruin the mood in here," Derrick replied.

"Mood, schmood." My earlier exhilaration over finally having a psychic lead had worn off. Tiredness was creeping in, one slow step upward at a time. "You mean elevators would ruin the creepy."

The catacombs were that in spades. The bones embedded in the walls were mostly human, since only young vamps left any behind when they died. Human victims, hundreds or maybe thousands, had been used to decorate the place their murderers were laid to rest.

That was just all kinds of wrong, with more wrong piled on top because human tourists came to gawp at the bones.

Yep, I was definitely moving into cranky pants territory.

"It is a place of death, Miss Jones."

"Says the vampire lord who can't drive worth a flip," I muttered.

"We didn't crash."

"We came close, dude. Pro tip: Corners? You slow down for them. The brake pedal is there for a reason."

Derrick laughed. "I'll try to remember that."

"You do that, Derryboy." I looked up and sighed. We weren't even halfway yet. "This is bull crap. Form a line, folks, and join hands. Discord Airlines is now boarding for takeoff."

I had to go back for Derrick's two minions, since they couldn't edge past the hounds. Enid and company joined us up top by taking their private, magical teleport.

Each hole in the wall opened onto a tunnel filled with deep alcoves and actual rooms. There were enough to slow even the hounds down, we learned.

Thanks to Logan's nose—he knew Mom's scent since he'd spent time around her—we could check each spot almost as quickly as the hounds did. I sent them to cover the right-hand side of the tunnel, and we two-legged types took the left.

The tunnels ranged from two to three miles in length, each. Halfway down the first, my headache returned. By the end of the third tunnel, I had the shakes and felt nauseated.

As we entered the fourth tunnel, I realized my coffee and toast Breakfast by Terra had been fourteen or fifteen hours previous. I hadn't eaten since, not a good thing considering I'd teleported three...no, four times?...and used my telepathy for scanning three hours straight. Oh, and finally got a rise out of my psychometry to boot.

Throw in the emotional ups and downs, a few adrenalin surges, and I was one sad, weak little panda.

Even so, I protested when we exited the fourth tunnel to see four vampires coming down the ledge, ready to take our places. "Mom could be in the next tunnel."

"If she is, they will find her," Derrick said.

"Discord, we're useless if we're exhausted. Might miss something." Logan rubbed his face with both hands. "And you're shaky. Have been for more than an hour."

"The creepy ambiance got to me," I lied, only to have him focus his bloodshot eyes on me, one eyebrow barely lifted. "Not gonna fall for that, huh?"

"Not even on your birthday."

"Damn."

Enid gently nosed my hand. "*I will bring her to you if she's found. Go and rest.*"

I had to look worse than I felt, if a hound was advising me to get some sleep. "Okay, fine, I surrender. Not sure I can make it down the steps though." My nausea rose at the thought. "Or teleport again."

"*I will take you and your companions down and return.*" Enid pushed by to put herself in the center of us. Derrick told his two minions to wait for the new arrivals; we laid hands on the hound, and were on the ground floor a blink later. All I saw of the hound was an afterimage, she left so quickly.

Logan drove, and Derrick claimed shotgun, leaving me to ride in back with Danielle. It wasn't until the vampire called ahead to arrange food and make certain rooms were ready for us that I realized I hadn't called to check on anyone. They probably understood, but it made me feel like crap. Again.

Back at Derrick's, I peeked into the library. Kate was gone, but Leglin was using one of the sofas as a bed. His huge paws rested on the coffee table. I smiled, noticing an inch or two of tongue protruding from his closed lips. He was snoring to beat the band. I shut the doors and followed the others to the dining room. Stone was there, serving himself from the buffet.

"I must take my rest now. Eat, drink, and take your own rest," Derrick said, inclining his head before leaving the room.

None of us felt like talking. Alanna, Soames, Gabriel, and Danielle's two cousins filed in a few minutes later to muted greetings.

I'd hit the point of having done without food long enough that my stomach was too mad to accept much. None of the shifters suffered the same problem. They loaded up on their first run down the buffet, and some were already sitting down with seconds by the time I'd finished my measly servings of Eggs Florentine and fresh cantaloupe, which was all my stomach deigned to accommodate.

I fell asleep at the table.

Eighteen

I woke up to way too much teal and a vague recollection of Logan carrying and tucking me into bed. Derrick needed to hire a new decorator. I sat up to look around, and yep, everything from carpet to wall paint was some permutation of teal. The wooden parts of the furniture were painted white, but that didn't do much to offset the horrid color choices of everything else. Not that I disliked teal, but I did prefer it to be less enveloping. No fireplace, but there was a bathroom.

After making use of it, I found my running shoes tucked under the side of the bed, their toes pointed out. I put them on and headed out the door, pausing to look over the railing at the main hall below. The now familiar bustle of people made it clear that Mom was still missing.

Enid and Leglin greeted me at the foot of the stairs. "Hey. Anyone feed you two yet?"

"*Dog food.*" Enid sniffed to express her opinion of that. "*We finished searching the catacombs hours ago. The dhampyr requested our assistance in searching other areas. I chose to report to you, but allowed the others to comply with his request.*"

"Thank you. You didn't find anything?"

"*The dhampyr has it. A necklace.*"

My heart jumped, and I dove into the crowd to look for Stone. It was more difficult that it should've been to find him, considering his height, but when I did locate him, Stone was sitting down at one of the tables. "You found a necklace?"

"Yes." He pulled it from the pocket of his jacket, in one of the ever present baggies. "Do you recognize it?"

"Gimme." It was Mom's, a delicate gold infinity charm on a simple box chain. My topaz birthstone winked from the cross of the symbol. I'd thought it was a bow when I was little. "My dad gave it to her when I was born."

Stone handed the bag over. "Can you use it?"

I already had the baggie opened. "About to find out."

The charm and chain spilled into my palm, and instantly, one of my abilities kicked in: Retro cognition.

I was in Mom's kitchen, watching as she spun around, her mouth falling open, when a vampire snapped the locks and shoved open the back door. The Chihuahuas, gathered around her feet, squealed and scattered around the end of the center island.

Red didn't run. He rose to all four paws, his hackles rising, and stalked forward to put himself between Mom and the vamp. His lips skinned back to bare his teeth, and the red pit growled.

"I suggest you leave before he attacks," Mom said.

A second vampire walked in behind the first. This one was taller. "I'll handle the dog."

Red's growl deepened, and I could see his muscles tensing.

"Get out of my house," Mom demanded. "Right now."

"My master wants to speak with you, Mrs. Jones."

Mom paled, only then realizing they were vampires. She glanced at the clock, but it was only a few minutes after six. There was a half hour or more before sunrise.

Red attacked, and she screamed, grabbing her favorite cast iron skillet off the stove top. The dog lunged upward, his head darting as he bit the taller vamp on each arm before trying for its throat. The shorter vamp slid past them, heading for my mother. She swung the skillet, but he caught her wrist and twisted, forcing her to drop it.

I hadn't even noticed it on the floor.

She sagged, forcing the vamp to bend over her since he didn't let go, and then shot upward, the top of her head colliding with his face. He fell backward, still holding her wrist. Red noticed. The dog backed a few steps before biting the downed vamp's arm, just above the wrist, and hard enough for me to hear bones snapping. Mom yanked free, nearly falling on her butt. Red lunged forward and up again, latching onto the upright vamp's hand and wrist. The vamp's other hand disappeared between them, and I dropped the necklace to cover my ears as Red's muffled scream of agony filled the air. Blood poured down.

"Red!" Mom cried, scrabbling for her skillet. His hind legs kicking, the dog refused to let go and the vampire swung him around, trying to sling the dog off. Blood sprayed everywhere.

The other vamp regained his feet just as Mom's hand closed around the handle of her skillet again. He slapped her across the face hard enough to knock her sideways, into the cabinet. Her eyelids fluttered, but didn't completely shut. Satisfied she was out of the fight, he turned and slipped in blood on his way to aid his fellow minion, who stopped trying to sling off Red.

Then he drove his clawed hand into the dog's throat and ripped it free. Red thrashed and went limp, his jaws still locked. A low, soft gurgle seeped from him, and that was it.

Hot tears were pouring down my face.

"It's not letting go."

"We're running out of time," the other said. He grabbed Red's body and pulled the dog away. The taller vamp yelled, holding up his maimed hand.

"You asshole."

"Shut up." The shorter one dropped Red's body and went for Mom. Grabbing her arm, he dragged her through the blood and past Red. My sobbing echoed hers as she stretched out her free arm, trying to touch the dog. She was yanked away before making contact.

The vision ended, leaving me on my knees in the main hall of Derrick's home. Logan knelt beside me, his arms around me as he quietly purred. Before I hid my face against his shoulder, I spotted Danielle glaring from the ring of silent bystanders.

She could go to hell.

I needed the comforting.

Logan and Alanna lifted me to my feet, while Soames and Gabriel shooed people away to give us room to walk. They took me to the dining room. By the time I was settled into a chair, I'd managed to stop the waterworks. "Sorry. I saw them take Mom."

And kill Red, but I didn't want to say it.

Stone, Danielle, and her two cousins had followed us. The dhampyr paused at the buffet to pour a cup of coffee, and brought it to me. "I think you should take a day off, and let us handle searching the remaining areas."

"No. Just give me a couple of hours. A little time alone, some food, and I'll be good to go." The amount of concern pouring from the four shifters—Logan, Alanna, Soames, and even Gabriel—was overwhelming. I didn't know what I'd done to earn it from them, not really. It wasn't as though I'd been much of a friend the past month or so, all wrapped up in my own business.

Their concern was offset by Stone's grim expression, and the bitter tang of Danielle's jealousy. Was it about Logan, or over how accepting of me some of the clan were? Didn't know. Wasn't likely to find out soon.

Stone had said "remaining areas", which meant we were almost finished with the Barrows. What if we didn't find Mom? I took too large of a drink and burned my tongue. "Ow. Seriously, let me get my head back in the game."

The dhampyr nodded. "Very well. I'll be in the main hall."

It proved a little harder to talk the rest into going, but at last, I had the dining room to myself. The buffet spread was dinner foods, aside from the coffee. I selected roast beef and a few veggies, ate, and then remembered I had phone calls to make. Not wanting to be interrupted, I teleported out to the gardens and found a little gazebo to sit in.

The first call: Dad.

"I'm sorry I haven't called before."

"Mr. Whitehaven's been keeping me updated," he said. "How are you holding up, kiddo?"

"I'm scared." I told him about the retrocog vision. "He told Mom his master wanted to talk to her about me. It is my fault, and I'm worried it'll happen again."

Dad sighed. "You can't let what's happened or what might happen keep you from living your life. I could walk out the front door and have something that fell off a plane land on my head. Life is full of risks. Everyone makes choices every day. Other people choosing to do evil isn't your fault."

He was wrong. Merriven wouldn't have known Mom existed if it weren't for me. I'd crossed him twice. "What if she's dead?"

Dad sucked in his breath and took several seconds before speaking. "Then you put all your energy into taking him down, so no one else loses someone to the bastard. But you do it smart, so that I don't end up losing you both."

"I want you to call Ronnie. I'll p...."

"Already called her. She's on vacation, but will come to ward both houses as soon as she gets back."

That gave me a measure of relief. "Good."

"Love you, honey. Call me when you can."

"Okay, love you too."

My next call was to David. He ignored my apology, assured me everyone was "well enough" and that they'd had no problems. He sounded a little disappointed about that. When the call ended, I simply sat there for a bit, breathing in and out, my eyes closed, trying to visualize a positive outcome. My cell phone rang, playing the first bars of "California Dreaming" and I knocked it off the bench in my hurry to answer it.

That was Mom's ringtone.

Snatching it up off the floor, I hit the accept button. "Mom?"

"She's here with me, and alive for the moment. Whether she remains so is entirely at your discretion." Merriven's voice raised goose bumps on my arms.

He could be lying. "Let me talk to her."

"Of course. Say hello to your daughter, Sunny dear."

"Cordi?" The voice was weak, but definitely my mother's.

"Mom. Are you okay? Has he hurt you?"

She didn't answer. Merriven had taken the phone away, and chuckled at my questions. "You sound like such a loving child, eager to see your mother safe."

I wanted to cuss him out for a few hours, but that probably wouldn't help Mom. "What do you want?"

"Excellent, you're ready to deal. A simple exchange, you for her, in two hours' time. We'll meet in the catacombs."

Damn it. "We've already looked there."

"Yes, but none of you found the entrance to my private retreat. I made certain it was closed."

Secret room, or... "Pocket realm?"

"Yes. Once here, you will ascend to the left side second level, and enter the eleventh tomb on the right. Walk past the dead man. The wall is an illusion. Walk through it, and continue walking until you see me. I'll release your mother then."

Yeah, right. Not that I said that out loud. "She doesn't know the Barrows. I need to bring someone to take her home." I held my breath, waiting for his answer.

"No."

Crap. With the firmest tone I could muster, I said, "No deal if I don't have a way to ensure she's really safe."

"My word's not enough?"

"Are you kidding me?"

Merriven growled. "I could drain her right now, while you listen to her beg for her life."

My hands began to shake. "Do that, and when you do see me, I won't be alone or only have one person with me. I'll come with a pack of elf hounds ready to rip you apart. They'll tear you to shreds, and then I'll burn every last scrap to ash."

Complete silence followed. I bit my bottom lip to keep from speaking, *Please don't hurt her* spinning over and over in my mind.

He finally drew a breath. "I'm going to enjoy drinking from you as slowly as possible."

"You're saying I can bring someone." Dang, I'd won a concession.

"Yes, one person. Not your hound. Make a wise choice for your mother's sake. You have two hours, and if you don't appear, she's dinner." He ended the call, and I dropped my phone again, shaking too much to keep hold of it.

I had two hours to save Mom, and not a clue where to start.

Or rather, whom to tell.

Nineteen

I wasn't fool enough to think I could win a fight against a master vamp with centuries of psychic practice. Which meant the person I chose to take Mom clear needed to be someone who wouldn't turn around and come back to help. Of course, a backup plan that would end in Merriven going down before he killed me wouldn't be a bad thing to have either.

All of that without endangering anyone else, or Mom even more. I had zero doubt Merriven would kill her if I showed up with a group instead of one person. I had less than two hours to figure it all out too, with not enough sleep and way, way too much stress over the past few days.

No problem.

Yeah, right. I kept drawing blanks on whom to tell. Who could I trust to keep their mouths shut and just follow the plan? Logan would go with me, but he'd want a plan in place so I'd have help once Mom was out of the danger zone. Soames would tell Logan. Leglin was out because I might need him as an emergency ride out.

Kate would stick Mom in a protective circle and come back to help, and might even be able to, but if she or anyone else were hurt, I'd never forgive myself.

Stone? I teleported back to the second floor and leaned on the railing to survey the dhampyr from above. If he kept quiet long enough to bring Mom to Derrick's estate...but if he didn't, it would ruin my one real chance of saving her.

That was the real problem: Picking someone who wasn't invested in my making it out alive in some fashion. Someone who wouldn't blab or try to talk me out of it.

I needed someone who didn't give a rat's behind about me.

Danielle crossed the main hall to speak to Logan. I studied her. She didn't care, and would probably be pleased if I dropped out of the picture. If I explained things right, she might even decide recovering my mother would gain her points with Logan. Jealousy could make people do anything.

Decision made, I wondered how to get her alone, but didn't need to. Luck was on my side as she headed for the stairs and began to climb them.

She made no effort to hide her annoyance when she spotted me waiting for her. Her upper lip curled as she vented a low hiss. "What do you want?"

"To ask if you'll help me get my mom back."

"I'm here, searching like everyone else." She walked past me and entered an open door. I followed, stepping into a bedroom done in shades of gray. It was more tastefully decorated than mine had been. Danielle tossed a sneer over her shoulder before entering the bathroom.

Parking myself to one side of the bathroom's door, I said, "My question wasn't general. Merriven contacted me a few minutes ago. He says he'll trade Mom for me, and I need someone who will bring her back here, to safety."

She didn't come rushing out to go yell the news. "And you're asking me. Why?"

"She doesn't know you. I have to know she's getting out of the way, and if I ask someone she knows, Mom might try talking them into going back to help me. I can't ask any of the vampires, not with her having been kidnapped and kept prisoner by one."

The toilet flushed, and a second later, water began running from a faucet. Danielle's voice rose over the sound. "You don't sound like you think you're going to survive the encounter."

"He's had centuries to learn how to control his abilities, and I don't even know how many he has." I wasn't going to tell her about the backup plan. The one I didn't actually have yet anyway.

"Yet you're going anyway, to save your mother." She appeared in the doorway, leaning against the frame opposite of where I stood, and studied my face.

"Wouldn't you, if it was your mother?"

Danielle looked away. "I'll go with you and bring her back here. When do we leave?"

"Meet me in the garden by that statue of vampire Cupid in an hour. That'll give us about thirty minutes to reach the meeting place. And thank you."

Her gaze returned to my face, her expression bland. "If you survive, you can thank me by being less friendly with our Protector."

"I'll do my best," I promised. "But I doubt it'll be an issue."

Pushing away from the door frame, she nodded. "The gardens in an hour."

"Yeah." I watched her leave and took a minute to savor the minor victory.

Now all I had to do was come up with a backup plan.

One hour later, I teleported to the gardens and quickly located Danielle by the statue. "We can't have anyone following us. We'll have to teleport."

"All right." She reluctantly extended her hand, and yanked it free from my grip once we appeared on the floor of the catacombs' cathedral area. "We searched here."

"There's a hidden portal to another pocket realm." I led the way to the stairs, hoping my backup plan worked. My purse was heavier than normal, and I'd finally hit on whom to ask to be my cavalry. It hadn't been as hard of a sale as I'd feared, when she'd first come to mind.

Yet I couldn't see or sense her near. What if she didn't show? I'd be up a creek without a paddle, that's what.

Worrying about it wouldn't do me any good. We'd reached the second level, and I led the way to the correct tunnel. Danielle followed without a word. Probably already anticipating a life free of me.

I counted, and stopped in front of the correct room. "This is it."

We both peered into the dimness of the tomb. Danielle said, "I don't see anything but a marble coffin."

"We have to go behind it to reach the portal. Come on." I entered the room and passed the coffin, heading for the shadowed wall behind it. She followed, hesitating when I did. The wall looked real. "It's an illusion."

I hoped, anyway, as I lifted my hand and pushed at the wall. My hand went through. "See?"

We walked through, finding ourselves in another tunnel. Kept walking until we entered a cavern that looked quite a bit like the catacombs' cathedral, minus the holey walls and ledges, and not nearly as well-lit.

Danielle stopped, and I followed suit. Merriven's voice slithered out of the shadows. "At last. Look how well you followed orders."

"Yeah, now where's my mom, you blood-sucking creep?"

The dim lighting became sunny brightness and I flinched, closing my eyes. When I opened them, the first thing I saw was Mom. She was on her knees in front of Merriven, gagged, with her hands tied behind her back. There was a dark bruise on her cheek from where she'd been slapped by one of her kidnappers. Otherwise, she appeared unhurt.

My knees shook but I stayed upright. "Let her go."

"Of course. I always keep my word." Merriven grasped Mom's arm and pulled her to her feet. She whimpered, and I wondered how long he'd made her kneel on the stone floor as he released her. She staggered toward us.

I met her halfway, Danielle on my heels. The first thing I did was remove the gag while checking her neck for bite marks. "Are you okay?"

"You shouldn't be here," she whispered while I began untying her hands.

"Don't worry about me." I kissed her unbruised cheek, wanting to hug her, but her arms were dangling and her wrists were raw from the rope. "This is Danielle. She's going to take you somewhere safe."

"But...."

"It'll be okay, Mom. Go with her." Merriven was smirking at us. "I'll see you in a little while."

Mom gazed at me for a second before nodding. "I love you."

"Love you too." I went ahead and hugged her, carefully, and didn't want to let go. Did anyway, since there was a vampire to deal with. "Danielle, get her out of here."

The shifter nodded, sliding her arm around Mom's back. I half-turned to watch them leave, keeping Merriven in view. Once they entered the tunnel, I turned to face him and cracked my knuckles. "All right, fang face, let's do this. I don't have all night."

He smiled, disturbingly handsome. His black hair was down past his shoulders, framing his high cheekbones, almond-shaped blue eyes, and just right chin: not too pointy, not too square. "The only place you have to be is at my side."

"I'll take 'highly unlikely' for two hundred, Alex." So he didn't want to kill me after all. Well, not without also turning me. Good to know, if only slightly less terrifying than dying or walking in here as blind as I had. "Hate to share this, but I kind of prefer men with pulses. Necrophilia isn't my bag."

"Ginger enjoyed my attentions." He walked around me in a wide circle, and I turned to keep him in sight.

"She hated your cold, dead guts with a purple passion."

His smile widened. "A master who can't control his fledglings isn't a master at all, Miss Jones."

What the hell did he mean by that? "Guess you're no master then, because you did a piss poor job of keeping her under control."

"Did I? 'Oh, Cordi, you have to help me. I can't live like this anymore. The things he makes me do...please, Cordi, I can't live with them. Help me.' Does that sound familiar, Miss Jones?"

Mouth open, I stared as his eyes began to turn red. "Did you really think she could do anything without my knowing?"

I closed my mouth and swallowed. Licked my dry lips. "Don't remember you showing up to drag her home."

"Why would I, when she was doing my bidding? It's unfortunate I was detained when you paid your final visit to her. If I hadn't been, you would already be mine."

"What are you saying?" I was afraid I already knew.

Merriven sighed. "I may have overestimated your intelligence. She was bait, Miss Jones. Bait for you."

My heart skipped a beat, my voice a whisper. "You made her tell me those things."

"It's a small matter to control a fledgling's mind or speak through her."

Oh my God. "She wanted out."

"No, Miss Jones, she wanted to stay young and lovely forever, and would have, if not for that unfortunate bit of timing."

I'd murdered my best friend, not helped her escape the horror she'd described to me so many times.

Twenty

"Poor little human child. Does it hurt to realize I was able to pull your strings and make you dance to my tune so easily? And not once, but twice now."

Was my therapist still practicing? I had the feeling I'd need to look her up in the near future. Then again, I'd never fully agreed with her on the "You're only responsible for yourself, your own actions and reactions" front. "You're ugly when you gloat."

Merriven cocked his head and said a word in another language. Two more vampires appeared from the shadows gathered behind him. One was a complete stranger, but the other was tall and missing three fingers.

The sight shoved all thoughts of socially acceptable therapy clear out of my head. "You killed my dog."

He glanced at Merriven, who gestured for him to respond. A wide grin cracked the vamp's face. "And you should've heard it scream when I tore its belly open." The scum sucker began hooting with laughter.

The noise of his hilarity grated against my grief, sparking rage.

With that rage came the urge to use the ability that scared me the most, because it was a double-edged sword: my empathic ability. It didn't just let me find out how others were feeling. I could twist its dial and make others feel anything I wanted.

Where this vamp was concerned, I wanted him to be as scared as my mom had been, and feel the pain Red had. I planted my hands on my fists. "How about we find out if your screams are as funny to me?"

He glanced again at his master. Merriven crossed his arms and raised an eyebrow as his minion lifted his hand to display his missing fingers. "Enough to regrow these?"

"No. You may break a bone, if you can."

I tensed, mentally scrambling to make the mental connections I needed. The vamp nodded, turned his head and smiled at me. He rushed forward, making it halfway to me before my telepathic spear slammed into his brain.

I let my retrocog memory of Henry Wilkins out of its box, and shoved it down the link with the full force of my empathic ability. My teeth gritted together as old Henry raised his gleaming straight razor. I'd gone through this memory hundreds of times, but it never seem to lose any of its power.

It was weird, seeing the memory from my mind apparently superimposed over the now motionless vamp. To know all he saw was Henry and that straight razor as it flashed down.

The vampire's first scream was pitiful, but the next rose in volume, bouncing off the cavern's walls.

I winced, instantly regretting the choice I'd made. Horrified I'd even thought of it in the first place. What the hell was wrong with me?

This wasn't justice, but torture. Intending to stop, I tried to shut down both my empathic ability and the telepathic link, only to discover I couldn't. While I wrestled to gain control of my abilities, the vampire's screaming continued, growing in volume and pitch. The sounds of it stabbed into my brain.

Unable to shut things down, my head pounding, and Henry Wilkins' gleeful smile burned into my brain, I just wanted it to end.

One way to do that. I reached for my pyrokinetic ability and blasted the vampire. He exploded into fine, white gray ash. His screams stopped. They still echoed in my ears and mind. I was on my knees, my heart thundering and stomach churning, as I stared at the mini-snowstorm of vampire ash. What had I done?

"I'll teach you to ignore that little voice," Merriven said at the same instant I realized his second minion wasn't beside him anymore.

Jamming my hand into my purse, I twisted and let myself fall onto my back, pulling out one part of my hastily made backup plan. The boss's wavy-bladed, demon-killing dagger glowed red as it sank into Minion Two's heart. Logan was definitely correct about vampires being demonic, because a gritty rain of vampire ash fell on me as the dagger's dragon-headed hilt made contact with his chest.

"Ugh." I rolled, spitting leftover vampire out, and came up on my hands and knees. The lights went out. Two down, one to go. The biggest, scariest one.

Or I could call it a night, teleport my sorry butt back to Derrick's, and let him come play Thunderdome with Merriven, while I looked for a new therapist.

A fantastic idea, and one that I immediately acted on. Nothing happened. "Oh, come the freak on!"

"Tsk, tsk." The sound fluttered from the darkness. "Are you experiencing technical difficulties?"

I stared so hard at the darkness surrounding me, little white dots appeared and began discoing all over. The sound of my breathing was magnified. Where was he? "No."

Merriven's laughter proved deep and surprisingly pleasant to the ears. Pleasant enough, I began to relax.

He wasn't going to hurt me. He wanted to give me the world; drop it into my hand like a giant, glistening dark pearl.

I nearly smiled before shaking my head hard enough to pop my neck. "You bastard."

He was inside my shield, in my head. I had no idea how he'd done it, or how long he'd been there. Forcing him out of my mind became Priority One.

Actually doing it was problematic, because he was inside my damn head. Now that I knew he was there, I could feel him watching my thoughts. He'd been in my memories too, leaving a faint trail of slime.

I screamed as Merriven grabbed my forearm and snapped both bones. The dagger thumped to the floor as he released me. He took a step back, and then kicked me in the ribs, driving out what little air there was in my lungs.

Nice of him to not use full vampire power on me. I only flew about five feet before hitting the stone floor on my uninjured, but soon to be bruised, side.

For several seconds, I couldn't move, overwhelmed by the furious cries of my ribs and arm. They hurt so badly, I couldn't cry or even breathe.

Couldn't do a damn thing, which was the perfect time for my cavalry to arrive, but nope. *Crap, I forgot....*

"No one can enter this realm. I closed the portal once the tiger and your mother left us."

I could've done without knowing that, and decided it was way after Get-the-Hell-Out-o'clock. Who needed to teleport if they had an elf hound on call? All I had to do was think....uh, what was my hound's name again?

"I'm afraid you won't be leaving anytime soon. You definitely won't be leaving as a warm-blooded human." The lights returned, and I blinked, because Merriven was standing right over me. His feet were planted on either side of my hips. I hadn't heard or felt him move. "Once you've learned your place, you'll begin your new existence in truth, as my little princess."

My voice was little more than a rasping wheeze. "So much wrong with that sentence."

"I thought every good little girl loved her daddy, and wanted to be his princess." Merriven shrugged. "Very well, I think I'll have Benjamin Thomas Jones brought in to be your first meal."

From the corner of my eye, I spotted the dagger, but didn't know how to reach it without him spying on my thoughts. The pain from my ribs and arm had died down a steady, throbbing wail, and I really didn't want to move. Being able to breathe was nice, though my breaths were shallow sips of air.

"I can take your pain away, or I can make it far worse." Merriven lowered himself to his knees, not touching me though he straddled my waist. Too injured to physically fight him off, I closed my eyes and grabbed hold of his presence in my mind.

It felt like cold snot. "Eww."

"Now that you have me, what do you plan to do?" Merriven's breath was cold too, brushing across my lips. Oh yuck, was he planning to kiss me? My disgust rose to heights I hadn't known were attainable, and when Merriven laughed at my reaction, I took advantage of his distraction to throw him off and away with my telekinesis.

He recovered too quickly, again blocking me from teleporting, and just as quickly, from setting him on fire. Well, now I knew for sure: Vampires did have way more and better control over their psychic abilities than I did.

Merriven totally Vadered me, using telekinesis to wrap an invisible hand around my throat and lift me to my feet. "I've grown weary of this. Come to me. It's time to meet your destiny."

I wasn't given a choice, the invisible hand growing, sliding down to grip my torso, and dragging me toward him. My arm felt as though two razors were sword-fighting inside it, and the stabbing pain in my side made it clear some of my ribs were broken. Unable to suck in enough air to scream, I squeaked like a rat caught on a glue trap. Was still squeaking when Merriven spun me around and grabbed a handful of my hair to wrench my head back. He sank his fangs into my neck and all I did was manage a louder squeak. He drank like a thirsty dog slurping down water on a hot day.

They say first-hand experience is usually better, but learning that it really doesn't take all that long for a vampire to drain a human's blood wasn't all that awesome. My vision darkened, and my mind grew fuzzy. I watched shadows gather on the cavern's ceiling, and then one crawling down the cavern's wall.

Oh, wait, that wasn't a shadow.

The flapping of wings sounded like thunder. Merriven snarled, ripping his teeth free of my neck, and was instantly too busy to do things like keep his TK hold on me, or maintain the telepathic link between us. I fell onto my side, feeling blood steadily escaping the wound in my neck, and for some reason, my thinking cleared enough to make a decision. I mentally shouted *"Don't kill him! Take him to Lord Derrick."*

The cavern abruptly went silent. The lights went out. I lay there, wondering if there was anything else I was supposed to do.

Call your hound.

What?

Who...Sal?

Call your hound. His name is....

"Leglin," I murmured before losing consciousness.

Twenty-one

"Would you hurry it up?"

Someone drove a knife into my arm. I shrieked, a high thin noise, and opened my eyes to be blinded by light.

"We're losing her."

"Do something." I knew that voice. Logan was there. I wanted to tell him that I was tired, and ask him to make whoever was poking at my neck to stop, but I couldn't see him.

"I am, you lump of fur. Clear."

Fire blazed through me, jolting my entire body. The light disappeared, but not for long.

Sal glimmered into existence. "Ooh, bet that hurt."

"Yeah." My jaws ached. So did my throat. "What was it?"

The wrinkle-faced god shrugged, and the tropical garden appeared around us. "One of those lightning boxes they use to zap hearts."

"Oh." I sank down onto a stone bench. "Crap, am I dead again?"

Sal chuckled. "No, you're experiencing a little electrical failure, and you seem to have misplaced quite a lot of blood."

Discord.

I looked around. "Who was that?"

"Someone who cares for you." He grinned. "By the way, good job, kiddo."

"You helped me."

He gave a slight nod, just a dip of his chin. "You were going foggy. Needed a nudge."

"Thanks." I took a moment to rummage around in my mind. No Merriven. "How did that bastard get into my head?"

"Your shield sucks."

Chin lowered, I glared at him. "That was helpful."

Sal's grin widened. "If you want to protect yourself from psychic sneak attacks, one wall isn't going to cut it. You need to build a series of walls. Actually, I recommend a maze, scattered with alarms and traps."

I slumped. "That sounds complicated."

"Yes, and complicated is exactly what will save your bacon." Sal sniffed, his upper lip curling. "Use your imagination, and spend time every day building it. Hide the map in the center, and create a guardian to defend it."

Discord.

"Who is that?"

Sal looked up at the sky. "Kids these days. You try to impart life-saving information, and they're distracted by text messages."

"Sorry. A maze, got it. Thank you."

His dark gaze returned to my face. "Good. Like I said, be creative with it. It's your mind, you can do anything in there you want. If you work at it every day, it'll eventually become real."

"Now you're confusing...."

Discord.

"Me." Geeze, who was that? Who was working on me while Sal and I had our little tête-à-tête? "How can something I imagine be real?"

"Mentally real, Discordia. It'll be real to you and anyone who tries climbing into your noggin. You'll always be shielded. You'll never have to rebuild it again, but," he lifted his forefinger. "A bit of redecorating from time to time wouldn't be amiss."

"Okay." I liked the parts about never being unshielded or having to rebuild my shield. "Anything else, or can I go now? I need to check on my mom."

Sal's face screwed up, his wrinkles tripping over each other. "The elf is tending your injuries, but you'll be weak for a while. Don't try using your abilities for a couple of weeks. They need time to recover too. If you do, you'll damage yourself."

"Why? I've never had...."

"Nearly every drop of blood drained and a master vamp renting space in your head? No, you haven't. Don't argue with your elder." He paused. "Use the time to remember you're not invincible. Let every ache and stab of pain remind you that you're human."

"Boy, that sounds like fun."

He scowled. "It's a lesson. Learn it."

"Yes, sir." I felt restless, and the voice rustled through the leaves, murmuring my name again: *Discord.*

"A little respect from my favorite psychic. It's a red letter day." Sal's scowl melted when he chuckled.

Favorite psychic. Why did that phrase drip ice water into my veins? Maybe because it meant I wasn't the only psychic he had an interest in, and why would a god be lurking around, giving psychics nudges and advice?

No good reason came to mind. To be honest, no bad ones did either. Didn't lay my sudden worry to rest though.

Discord.

I stood. "I have to go."

"Yes, you do. I'll be in touch, kiddo." Sal waved his hand and everything went dark.

"Urgh." I clawed at my mouth, choking on whatever filled my throat. My frantic movements caused dull pain and brought people running.

Alleryn's face swung into view and he grabbed my wrist. "Stop that. You can breathe, you little twit. It's called a breathing tube for a reason. I'll remove it if you'll be still."

I narrowed my eyes, resorting to gagging to get him to let go and pull the damn thing out. Which he did. It proved to be a less-than-pleasant experience. My throat burned as I gulped in air. "Mom?"

Logan appeared on the other side of the bed, and touched my shoulder. "She's safe. Danielle brought her to Derrick's. Sunny's asleep in the next room."

Thank God. My voice sounded as though someone had sanded my vocal cords. "Merriven?"

"Not dead yet, for some reason, but he's in custody. Derrick's custody."

She'd listened. Good, even if I didn't understand the impulse that had me yell at her not to kill him. I'd figure it out later. There were more important questions. "Where?"

Logan frowned. "Merriven?"

"No." Gah, this conversation was going to take forever, with the ban on using my abilities. Telepathy would've been easier.

"Oh. This is Alleryn's clinic in the sidhe. We brought you here."

"We?"

Logan nodded. "When Danielle came in with Sunny, and they told us where you were, I knew if things went bad, you'd call for Leglin. I asked him to take me with him."

"Thanks."

He smiled. "Just returning the favor."

A broken arm, three cracked ribs, the hole in my neck, and nearly successful exsanguination were my total injuries.

I slept all day Saturday, and through the night, waking Sunday morning to an obscenely cheerful Alleryn walking in with a tray and IV bags. "Good morning. How are we feeling today?"

"Don't know about you, but I'm hungry, my ribs are stabbing me, and my arm hurts. This itches." I pointed at the bandage on my neck. "And I want a bath."

"Eat your breakfast." Alleryn deposited the tray on the rolling table and pushed the table in place over the bed. He began changing the IV bags, one of which was blood.

"Where does an elf get a supply of blood from for his private clinic?"

"A pushy, growly bodyguard." He checked the lines. "Just finished drawing it. He's eating. You should be too."

I lifted the cover from the plate. Cheesy quiche, bacon, and paper-thin slices of honeydew melon rolled into bite size pieces. "Yum. How's my mom?"

"Better than you are. She didn't break anything." The elf pulled a chair over to my bedside and sat. "Dehydration, hadn't been fed during her captivity, bruising and abrasions from being restrained. She's exhausted."

Fork halfway to my lips, I looked at him. "Dehydration?"

"Not from being fed on. She wasn't bitten. They didn't give her enough water." He pointed at my breakfast. "She's remarkably unharmed, physically, considering the circumstances."

I took my waiting bite. The quiche was wonderful, a blast of sharp cheese with hints of spinach and herbs. "Mentally?"

Alleryn smiled. "It was a traumatic experience, but she's in good spirits. Sunny is a resilient woman."

"That's awesome." Best news I'd had in a few days. "Thank you."

"You're welcome."

"How much do I owe you?"

Alleryn's expression turned solemn. "That's a dangerous question to ask an elf."

"But a necessary one."

He nodded. "Yes."

"So?" I prompted, steeling myself for the answer.

"I think the highest of prices: trust and friendship."

I ate a few bites, trying to think my way through that. "Why those?"

"You are one of a small number who tread the line between humanity and supernaturals, as we've been collectively labeled. You're one of the few of those in this city with true power." A faint smile appeared on his face. "You also possess a good heart. I would rather be counted as a trusted friend to you than an annoyance or enemy."

Take that at face value, or ask more questions? He had done a lot for me in the past, as Dr. Allen. Kate was dating him, and her familiar was okay with it. "You're not going to ask me to kill anyone, are you?"

"I have no such plans."

"Okay, we can be friends then."

Alleryn chuckled. "Wonderful."

The requested bath didn't happen because I fell asleep after breakfast, and didn't wake until a gorgeous, raven-haired elf woman brought my dinner. "Thank you."

She inclined her head with a small smile, and left. I wondered if she understood or spoke English while checking my tray.

"Hey."

Looking up from the artful arrangement of sliced prime rib, snow peas, and Julienne potatoes, I found Logan standing in the doorway. "Hi. Want to keep me company while I take my medicine?"

"Sure." He smiled and walked in to sit down. "How are you feeling?"

"Tired." I held up my left hand in illustration. "And shaky. But my throat feels better."

"Good. After you eat, Sunny wants to see you. I'll help her walk over."

That didn't sound good, after Alleryn's report. "Is she worse?"

"She's doing great, but a little shaky too. I'll feel better, being on hand just in case."

"Oh, okay." I dove into the meal, eager to see Mom. "I don't mean to be rude, but shouldn't you be with Terra?"

Logan grinned. "Teague hasn't seen any signs of other shifters, and your Pit Crew has been guarding the shop's door during business hours. Terra's having a lot of fun there, and David said he didn't mind them staying longer."

Well. Good to know I wasn't wrong about the safest place to stash people. "I owe David big time."

"He's a good guy."

Good night, the prime rib parted under my fork like butter, and was melt-in-my-mouth perfection. I swallowed, wondering if I could ask for seconds. "Alleryn roped you into donating again. I'm sorry."

"Don't be. You needed it." His dark green, gold-flecked gaze slid to the doorway. "You have more of my blood than your own right now."

"Geeze, then how are you even wal...," I closed my mouth, realizing what a stupid question it was.

His grin returned. "By eating roughly my own body weight. Body weight as a tiger."

Asking for seconds didn't seem like a big deal after that.

When Logan left to bring Mom to see me, I spent the time thinking. Regardless of what everyone said, what had happened was my fault.

I'd always worried my job would end up endangering my family, and now it had. Twice in only a couple of months.

Mom came in, her arm tucked in Logan's as he escorted her to the chair. "Yell when you're ready to go back."

"All right, thank you." She looked tired, her eyes bloodshot and the skin under them dark, but she was smiling. He shut the door as he left. Mom leaned forward, placing her hand on my arm. "They said you were all right. You don't look all right."

"I'm okay." I suddenly wanted to cry, seeing her. Being told she was safe wasn't the same thing as seeing it with my own eyes. "I'm going to talk to Mr. Whitehaven as soon as I can. Work something out so I can quit."

She blinked. "Why would you do that?"

"Mom, seriously?"

She shook her head, her brow furrowing. "I don't want to be the reason you quit the job you love."

"You aren't. I mean, not exactly."

"If you quit because of what happened, and what nearly happened to your brother Sean, evil wins." She patted my arm. "It's your decision, but the world has, and always will need people to fight against evil."

I thought she'd be relieved by my decision. "You don't want me to quit."

"I'm proud of what you've decided to do with your life and your gifts. You're young, and will be able to help a lot more people."

"I wasn't there to help you or Red. You wouldn't have needed help if it weren't for me."

"Oh, Cordi," she sighed. "If I died in a car accident on my way to work one day, would you blame yourself for not being there too?"

Probably, which would be dumb. "That's not the same thing."

"Bad analogy." She smiled. "You're not the only person who faces this. Don't you think police, judges, and others like them worry about their jobs affecting their families? Yet they still do their jobs. They keep fighting evil."

Much as I didn't want to admit it, she'd made a good point. "Let me think about it."

"You do that." Mom rose from the chair and leaned over my bedside to kiss my forehead. "I love you. See you tomorrow."

"Okay. Love you too." I heard Logan say something as she stepped out into the hallway, leaving me to decide what to do about my life.

Mom wasn't my only visitor that evening. An hour after sunset,

Logan tapped on my door and asked, "Are you awake?"

"Yeah." Still needed a bath too. "Come on in."

He opened the door. "Lord Derrick's here to see you."

Wasn't that interesting? A vamp come a visitin' to a fairy mound. Sidhe. Whatever. "Okay."

My "bodyguard" stepped aside to allow Derrick to enter the room. The slim, boyish-faced vampire lord held a giant bouquet of mixed flowers in an indigo-colored, glass vase.

"You brought me flowers?"

Derrick froze, his smile slipping. "Isn't that the proper protocol when visiting someone in a hospital? Your mother didn't seem to find it odd."

Whew, if he'd brought Mom flowers too, it wasn't a romantic gesture. "Sorry, I was surprised. They're beautiful. Thank you."

His smile returned as he crossed the room to place the flowers on the bedside table. "You're welcome. May I?" Derrick gestured at the chair.

"Sure." As he sat down, I said, "Logan told me you have Merriven in custody."

"Chained in silver. It weakens us."

"I know." Thank you, Soames. "What are you going to do with him?"

The vampire chuckled. "Use him for the gift he is."

"Come again?"

"He will be our public peace offering. Picture this, Miss Jones." Derrick lifted his hands and spread them wide. "The council has been diligently working to weed out those of our people who fail to abide by our new laws. One member, Lady Esme, grew suspicious of some fellow council members after a member of her family saved a human from being killed."

I held up my good hand to stop him. "Got the picture. Jump the part where you start lying."

He laughed. "The only change is to the intent behind the reasons you were hired. Instead of simply to solve the murders of a few council members, it was to investigate whether there was a conspiracy in place, vampires aiding each other in covering up their murders."

Which meant the story would work, since ninety-nine percent of it was truth. "Okay."

"We'll be able to reveal the discovery of the bodies, and see that they're identified and returned to their families for proper burial. We'll try, sentence, and execute Merriven for the crimes, as the last remaining member of the conspiracy. His death will be a warning to others who may not be following the law, and a sign to the humans that we're sincere about co-existing peacefully."

"Bad guys dead, families no longer wondering what happened to their loved ones, and the council gets credit for being serious about not killing humans for food." I nodded and narrowed my eyes at him.

"What's the catch?"

"While we'll make every effort to suppress the information, it's likely the press will discover which agency we hired, and thus, your name."

"Mr. Whitehaven won't like that." Hell, neither would I, having seen what the media did to some people.

Derrick crossed his ankles, leaning back in the chair. "I've discussed the matter with him, and pointed out that it was highly unrealistic to expect to remain 'under the radar' forever. Sooner or later, one of you would end up solving a case like this."

What was it with everyone making points I couldn't reasonably argue with today?

Twenty-two

Mindful of Sal's advice, I took two weeks of sick leave once Alleryn released me from his clinic. Whatever was left of my injuries at the end of that time, I'd let my auto-healing ability take care of.

I spent time every day building the mental maze he'd suggested. Not the easiest of tasks, but a conversation with Jo resulted in Tonya bringing home a book on mazes from the Blue Orb. Studying it helped a lot.

Other than that, I spent too much time napping, trying to decide if I would keep my job, and watching daytime television.

That last was what I was doing when someone pulled up, parked, and came to the door about a week after I'd come home.

When the doorbell rang, none of the large dogs so much as twitched an ear, even when the Chihuahuas charged the entryway, their cacophony of shrill barks shattering the quiet.

I moved enough to see through the sheers covering the living room window, and saw Nick's truck. "Come in!"

He came inside, careful to avoid letting anyone out as the little dogs attacked the cuffs of his jeans. It took him a few minutes to walk to the other side of the coffee table without stepping on any small bodies. Once there, he shoved his hands into his pockets. "Hey."

"Hi." We gazed at each other, and his eyes flicked to the bandage on my neck and cast on my arm.

"Mr. Whitehaven told me what happened when I gave my notice. Is your mom okay?"

"She says she is."

Nick's gaze moved to the two remaining members of my Pit Crew. "I'm sorry for your loss. It hurts to lose a pack member."

"Thank you," I said for them.

He looked at me. "From what he said, you almost died."

"It was close." Man, this was uncomfortable. "But everything worked out all right."

Nick nodded, his lips compressing. "You were lucky. Again."

I was too tired to feel any anger at his assessment. "I had a plan, and it worked."

"You almost died, Cordi. That's not really great planning." He pulled his hands out and lifted them, palms toward me. "Sorry. I didn't come here to argue."

Fine by me. "Why are you here?"

That was apparently a bad question, because his jaws clenched before he ground out, "To make sure you were okay."

"I'm good."

"And to see if we can start over."

Oh, so not what I wanted to deal with right now. "We don't see the same future ahead for us."

Nick shook his head while sinking down to a crouch so that we were sort of on eye level with each other. "No, you don't think the future I see is possible for you."

"I know it's possible."

His eyes widened. "Then why...."

"It's possible if I give up everything I have and do."

"Don't you think that might be a good idea, after this?" Nick waved his hand at me, indicating the bandage and cast. "To quit and get away from the danger?"

Somehow, his question made the decision I'd been fretting over simple. I wasn't going to quit my job. "The only way I might do that is if I loved you."

Nick flinched. "And you don't."

"No. I care for you a lot, and I think you're a good person. We've had fun together, but we argue all the time because you don't like the way I do things, or the choices I make." I had to take another deep breath. "You're not the right guy for me, Nick, and I'm not the right girl for you."

"I love you."

"I'm sorry."

He rose to look down at me. Bone's ear twitched, and I laid my hand on his scarred head. Nick's eyes followed the movement. "So that's it?"

"Yes."

"No regrets at all? We're just done?"

"The only regret I have is that I hurt you. I never meant to do that."

He nodded, looking down at the Chihuahuas still mauling the cuffs of his jeans. "Okay. Maybe we'll see each other around."

"Maybe." I sort of hoped not. "Good-bye, Nick."

"Bye." He didn't look at me, just waded free of the Chihuahuas and left. The roar of his truck's engine followed the soft click of the front door shutting, but he didn't peel out while driving off.

I let out a long, hard sigh and Bone moved his head to rest his chin on my thigh. *"You humans have a saying: You're better off without him."*

"Maybe he's better off without me."

Bone grunted.

I began scratching behind the stub of his missing ear. "Maybe you guys would be too."

Both pits raised their heads to look at me, and Diablo growled. *"So now you're going to throw us out?"*

"Of course not. I think my dad...."

"No." Diablo lurched to his paws, shoving his muzzle into my face. *"You promised we had a home with you. Said we were your pack."*

Bone sat up, shoving Diablo back. *"You did. We don't want to live with someone else."*

"Okay, okay! Geeze, guys. Calm down." Guess their reaction settled the matter. I threw my arms around both their necks and squeezed them together for a hug. "We're family."

My phone rang. I released them, Diablo grumbling about my cast touching him. "Hello?"

"Hi. It's Terra. I have my own phone now." Her pleasure over her news came through loud and clear in her bubbly-toned voice.

"Awesome, what kind did you get?" We talked phones for a few minutes, until the teen cleared her throat.

"I have something important to ask you."

Uh-oh. The memory of hearing her tell Logan she hoped I'd help her pick her mate rose. I didn't want to do that. Being a psychic didn't mean I'd be a good matchmaker. "Okay."

Terra sucked in a breath and blurted out, "We want to adopt you into the clan. Would you be interested in that?"

So not what I'd expected to hear. "I'm sorry, what?"

"You're already known publicly to be our ally, and Logan donated a lot of blood, which sort of makes you clan anyway. I mean, sharing blood leaves a kind of residue. People are going to think you're clan."

"Ah," she was going way too fast for me. "What kind of residue?"

"Like a combination of magic and spirit. It'll show in your aura. People who are sensitive to auras might think you smell like a tiger, or that you're a shifter."

And no one thought to mention that to me before now? "I see."

"Are you mad? Don't be mad. It'll wear off if we don't have the ceremony."

"Logan saved my life. I'm far from mad," I assured her.

"Oh, good."

"What does the ceremony do? Permanently glue the residue on my aura?"

"Basically, and you should be able to sense us before you see us, and the same for us where you're concerned."

That could be useful. Soames would be going to work at Arcane Solutions, and since I was going to stay there, he'd probably be assigned as my new partner now that Nick had quit. "Okay, are there any downsides here?"

"I don't think so. I mean, not any that are different from you being our ally," Terra replied.

I stroked Bone's head. "What about responsibilities?"

"That has been harder to figure out. Logan said it wouldn't be right to ask you and expect you to change your life to how we do things, with the living close together and tithing your paycheck into the clan pot."

Logan was right about that, but I didn't say anything other than "Uh hmm."

"Plus, he said the dogs might not like living in close quarters with us twenty-four-seven." Terra paused. "This sounded simpler in my head to explain."

I had to laugh at that. "Let me try to do a short version: Nothing really changes except for my being permanently tagged with clan 'residue'. I keep being your friend and helping out like I have been."

"Yes, but we'll have a deeper connection, too. You'll be clan. Um, do you want time to think about it?"

"No."

"Oh. Okay, I'm sorry...."

I had to laugh, wincing when my ribs complained. "I don't need time to think about it. You guys have been great friends, even when I haven't been a good one back. I've felt more at home with you than I have with any other supes. If you want to adopt me into the clan, my answer's yes."

"Awesome!" she shrilled. "Cool, can we do it tomorrow night? The ceremony, I mean?"

"I guess, but I'm still injured. Kind of get tired easy."

"Don't worry, we'll take care of everything, all you have to do is show up. Wait, I'll send someone to pick you up at seven. I have to go. Have a lot of stuff to do. See you tomorrow. Oh, this is awesome!" Terra ended the call, and I put my phone down, shaking my head and grinning.

Mom and Tonya brought home a selection of Chinese food for dinner. None of us wanted to be in the kitchen much, even though a professional cleaner had removed all signs of Red's death. I hadn't found out who had arranged for that, but did know that Dad had called someone in to repair the back door.

We pulled the big, square decorative pillows off the furniture to use as seats, and settled around the coffee table. "I won't be home for dinner tomorrow."

"Oh?" Mom passed a carton of shrimp fried rice to me. "Why not?"

"Terra called. They want to adopt me into the clan, and I said yes."

"Building bridges in the supe community. Go, Cordi." Tonya grinned at me before diving into her chicken lo Mein.

I hadn't thought of it like that, and smiled back. "Guess so."

"As long as it feels right to you," was Mom's opinion. The conversation turned to Tonya's studies and the upcoming Halloween party at the center.

Twenty-three

When the doorbell rang the next evening, I half-expected it to be Logan who'd come to pick me up, but it was Soames. "Hi. I had no idea what to wear."

He laughed. "Jeans are fine."

"Cool." That's what he had on, along with a red t-shirt and jean jacket. I'd picked jeans, and a beige, cowl-necked sweater. The nights tended to be chilly, even if the days were still warm. "Let me grab a jacket."

"Okay." He waited while I did that and petted each dog who'd followed me to the front door. Which was basically all of them. At least I didn't have to bend to pet Leglin.

Once we were in his truck and on our way, Soames said, "I really appreciate you talking to Mr. Whitehaven."

"You're welcome." He was a heck of a lot easier to work with than Nick. "We're going to have fun working together. We make a good team."

He grinned. "I thought so."

"Any leaks yet?" I asked, referring to the media. He shook his head. "Good. But it is working, right? I haven't seen anything on the news about about protestors or attacks on vamps."

"Seems to be. Lord Derrick's a good choice for spokesperson. He looks harmless."

That struck me as funny, and my ribs complained when I laughed. "Ow. Yeah, I guess he does."

We talked about work for the rest of the drive, and eventually made it out past the city limits to a fenced pasture.

"This is our temporary gathering place. The rancher who owns it lets us rent it," Soames explained while parking among other trucks along the fence line. "Not much grazing for his cattle here."

"Cool." I could see some lights not far away, and the intermittent breeze carried the murmur of voices. The gate was open, and we made the short trek to where the rest of the clan was.

Terra and Alanna met us, greeting me with gentle hugs. The blonde teen whipped a marker out of her back pocket. "Can I sign your cast? I learned people do that."

"Sure." I held up my arm, and she stuck her free hand under to help before drawing a flower on the cast. She added "Heal fast" and her name.

"There's food," she informed me. "I hope you're hungry."

"Starving."

The two women led me to a large tent, the front of which was mosquito netting. Tables covered with food waited inside, along with lines of people piling their plates high. More proof that shifters ate like there was no tomorrow. Smiling faces greeted us, some people saying "hi" while others just nodded.

The general atmosphere felt calm and happy. I relaxed, selecting grilled chicken, a baked potato, fried okra, and a slice of chocolate cake. Terra carried our plates, leaving me to handle my plastic cup of tea. Outside the tent, picnic tables dotted the immediate area. During the day, there wouldn't be any shade, but it was pretty pleasant at night.

I looked around as we walked over to a table, and didn't see Logan anywhere. However, I did see Danielle, who glared back before turning away. Right, joining the clan wasn't exactly conducive to not trying to be friendly with Logan anymore. Oh, well.

We ate, and Terra informed me they'd had the event semi-catered. People began drifting off beyond the lit area as I finished my last few bites.

"If you're done, let's go to the circle," Terra said.

"Okay." I ran my tongue over my teeth, as we left the table, hoping there weren't bits of chicken caught between them. Those still hanging around followed us. I still hadn't spotted Logan, and wondered where he was.

The circle was sort of a double one, with rocks marking its boundaries, and people standing a few deep the full way around its interior perimeter. Terra and Alanna led me through them, right to the center where a slab of sandstone sat. It was covered in a dark cloth, a brass bowl, candles, and other things lying on top of it. One of those things was a knife, its obsidian blade dull in the starlight.

Terra coughed, a deep grunt of sound that instantly silenced everyone. "We are gathered tonight to consider a new addition to our clan. I ask who among you will stand before us with this woman?"

"I will." Logan's voice. He slipped past a few people and crossed the intervening space to stand on my left, offering me a smile.

"As will I," Alanna said. She was already standing on my right, between Terra and me.

"And I." Soames cleared the crowd and lined up next to Logan.

"I will stand with her." Gabriel joined us, standing next to Soames.

"I will too." The woman who came forward wasn't someone I'd met yet. She had a pretty, friendly face, freckles, and red hair bright enough to know it was red in spite of the lack of good light. We traded a smile as she walked over.

Terra lifted her hands. "Does anyone object to the inclusion of Discordia Angel Jones into our clan?"

"I object." Not Danielle, which I expected the minute I heard Terra's question, but her barrel-chested cousin. He took a step forward. "She's human, not tiger."

The red-headed woman spoke up. "There is tiger in her aura. I see and smell it."

"She can't shift." He crossed his arms as though that settled the matter.

"Doesn't need to, in order to defend clan and Queen," Logan said.

The cousin wasn't ready to back off. "This is against tradition."

"We live in a new world now, and some traditions will change." Alanna stared at him. I tried not to fidget. "She has been friend and ally to the clan. Has twice helped prevent others from taking our Queen."

A murmur of agreement rose, and Danielle's cousin twitched before dropping his arms to his sides. "I withdraw my objection."

"Then let us begin." Terra picked up the knife and cut her thumb pad, directing the resulting drip of blood into the bowl. Alanna did the same before they walked away from the altar to collect blood from those around us.

It took a while before they came back to us. I managed to keep from hissing as Terra drew the blade across my thumb. Once the others standing with me donated their drops, Terra replaced the bowl on the altar.

She and Alanna began a singsong chant while lighting the candles, and moved on to adding the waiting herbs and other things to the bowl. Logan moved a little closer to me, his voice low. "They're asking for the gods' blessings on your inclusion. Each item is a representation of the things important to us, and a sacrifice to them."

I nodded and whispered, "Have the gods ever said 'no way'?"

He chuckled. "No."

I hoped I wouldn't be the first one the gods said no to. The women's voices rose and fell, and finally fell silent as Terra dropped the last thing, which looked like dirt, into the bowl and stirred it with the knife. I wasn't remotely prepared for the sudden volcano of multicolored smoke that erupted from the bowl. She hadn't dropped a lit match into it.

Logan steadied me with his hand across my lower back as my gaze followed the smoke upward. It formed a column and slowly began to revolve. Tiny green sparks began jumping out of the bowl, dancing free and pulling thin threads of smoke after them.

At some unknown signal, the green sparks darted away from the column, each one halting over someone's head. I looked straight up to find one over mine too. They'd pulled and separated the smoke out into a net of sorts over the circle. Just as suddenly as the smoke had appeared, the sparks all dove downward. Mine landed somewhere above my eyes.

It didn't hurt, but I couldn't close my eyes. The sparks seemed to funnel the smoke into each of us, and I wondered if everyone felt the same flush of warmth I did.

Or if they could see the circle of spectral tigers pacing above us. Hundreds of them, most the usual orange, black, and white, but a few black tigers, and white ones too. I didn't want to blink, afraid of missing a second of the awe-inspiring sight.

They began to fade away as the last of the smoke slid its way into people, and were gone as the green sparks flickered out. I lowered my head, blinking to relieve the strain of keeping them wide open, as Terra shouted, "It is done."

With the ceremony over, party time began. People streamed back to the tent and tables, laughing and talking as they went. Logan noticed I'd grown a little shaky and offered his arm. "Thanks."

"No problem. By the way, this is Moira." He meant the red-headed woman, who fell in step with us on my other side.

"Hi. Thanks for, uh," I lifted my cast slightly, not sure how to complete what I'd been saying.

"You're welcome." Moira radiated good humor and warmth. "I bet that was strange for you."

"The smoke startled me, but the rest was cool, especially the tigers."

Logan stumbled slightly and Moira's eyes widened. They both asked, "Tigers?"

Maybe I shouldn't have said anything about them. "Um, yeah. Kind of ghostly looking, in the sky over us?"

Before either could respond, a scream came from somewhere near the tent. Logan unwound his arm from mine, pointing at Moira. "Stay with her."

She nodded, and he rushed away. I followed her to the closest picnic table, and we climbed onto it for a look. Moira hissed. "Those damn outsiders."

Mega Douche was plowing through the clan, his followers on his heels. I spotted Terra being herded toward us, Logan at her back, but then she turned and darted around him, avoiding everyone who reached to stop her.

She shifted, her clothing tightening and tearing before falling free. There were only a few seconds to admire her black-striped, white figure before she leaped at Mega Douche. He actually punched her in her tiger face, an uppercut that knocked her away.

Meanwhile, others were shifting to tiger, including Logan, who charged toward the oversized enemy. But before he reached Mega Douche, who was now a gigantic tiger, a white streak struck the enemy leader. He and Terra rolled a few feet, and she sprang free before Mega D wrapped his heavy front legs around her.

Thwap, thwap, thwap! She began pounding away at his head and face, her claws extended and drawing blood with each blow.

"Thatta girl! Show him who's boss!" I cheered, wrapping my good arm around my ribs. "Ow."

Thwap, thwap, thwap. I squinted at Terra. Her white fur seemed to be brighter than before. "Um, is she glowing?"

"Yes." Moira bounced up and down, before a fierce grin appeared on her face. "She is."

A final blow from Terra toppled Mega D onto his side. She roared, and I gaped as tigers became humans again, all except Terra. Even those who were unconscious. At least, I hoped they were only unconscious.

The shifters closest to Terra dropped down to their knees, bowing their heads, and those behind them followed suit, until the only people standing were Moira and me.

I realized what had happened.

The White Queen had come into her own.

Terra hadn't killed Mega Douche. In spite of the number of naked people around, I made my way over to him to check once Moira helped me down from the tabletop.

He was conscious, lying on his side and curled into fetal position. That made it easier to ignore the fact that he was naked as a jaybird. So did the bright pink lines crisscrossing his face and scalp, and the blood-seeping puncture wounds dotting his face and neck. "How bad are you hurt?"

"I'm healing."

I crouched down. "I didn't help this time." He glared back. "She kicked your ass, dude, and she's only a teenager. Just sayin'."

He grunted, uncurling enough to roll forward and push up until he was resting on hand and hip. I kept my eyes on his face, trying not to notice his now-exposed junk lying right at the periphery of my view. The whole shifter nudity thing was a little too much for my delicate sensibilities. "She's come into her power."

"Yeah, that's what I thought happened. It'd probably be a good idea for you and your buddies to call it a night. Might want to think long and hard about coming after her again too. She may decide you're too irritating to live." I shrugged, rising to dust off my jeans, and added, "You might even consider getting the hell out of Santo Trueno. Just sayin'."

He stood up too, and I couldn't avoid a full-body look while lifting my gaze to his face. Holy crap, he was scary big all over. I hoped no one noticed my face turning red. "What if I don't?"

"Then I guess you deserve whatever you get, dude." With that, I turned my back on him and walked away, trying to pretend I was blind.

Way too many naked people around for my comfort. Way, way too many.

I made an about-face to hide in the tent when I realized most of them were heading the direction I wanted. If the cars were that popular now, I could make my own way home soon. No one else was in there, and it seemed like a good place to wait until the clothing impaired became unimpaired.

"Discord?"

"Yes?" I didn't turn around to look at Logan.

"Are you all right?"

"Yeppers. Hiding out with the food for now."

"Why?"

"Naked people."

"Oh. Give me a few minutes. I'll get dressed and come back."

"Actually, I'm kind of ready to go home, if that's okay." I hadn't realized how tired I was until then.

"It's okay. Not sure...what do you want to do? Close your eyes and let me lead you?"

Sounded like a future funny story in the making. "Yes, let's do that."

He laughed. "Okay, close your eyes and turn around."

I did, and he walked over to take my hand. "Here we go."

"Bet you think I'm being silly about the nudity."

"Being raised differently isn't silly," Logan said. "We usually don't run around without clothes anyway."

"Oh. So, Terra's officially Queen now?" I'd missed her eighteenth birthday.

"Yes."

"Which means she doesn't need bodyguards all over the place to go somewhere?"

Logan's fingers tightened on my hand. "Well, she should always have someone close by. Why?"

"I missed her birthday party. Thought I'd do something to make up for it after my cast is off." After I could use my abilities again.

"She'd like to spend some time with you."

It wasn't exactly a yes, but it wasn't a no either. "I'll figure something out and let you know."

"All right. We're almost to the gate."

"Hey, Logan." That was Soames. "Terra wants to talk to you."

We stopped, and I heard Logan sigh. "All right. Discord's ready to go home."

I thought about telling him I could wait, but kind of wanted to take a pain pill and pass out. "Thanks. See you."

"Yeah." He brushed his cheek against mine, putting a smile on my face, and released my hand.

"Why are your eyes closed?"

I sighed. "Naked people."

Soames didn't get it. "And?"

"Just lead me to your truck, and if you don't have clothes on, could you find some? I don't want to explain to my mom why you're naked when you drop me off."

He laughed. "I have clothes on, come on."

And away we went.

Twenty-four

After the excitement of Ceremony Night, I made a determined effort to chill out for a while. A couple of days before I was due back at work, I decided I'd been sitting on my rear end for long enough, because of my car.

My poor baby was covered in dust from being parked. Though it was mid-October, the day was hot enough to slip into a bikini and drag out everything needed to wash a car.

I mixed carwash liquid with water in a bucket and started with the roof. Barely twenty minutes of scrubbing later, I was panting like an overheated dog. "This is what I get for being a couch potato."

With a sigh, I rinsed the roof off and sat down in a lawn chair. My car looked worse than before I'd started.

While I sat gazing in disgust at the mess I'd made, Logan pulled up at the curb.

Instant embarrassment. My black bikini had seemed perfect car-washing garb, but it also showed off my ghost white skin from the neck down. My only consolation was the fact the tan on my arms, neck, and face had faded a lot, so that I wasn't noticeably two-toned.

Logan walked around his truck, looking at the bucket, towels, and hose. "Hi."

"Hey." That's me, the brilliant conversationalist.

"Need some help?"

Hm, hot guy offering to wash my car. I went with the intelligent response. "Yes, please. I guess I'm still not one hundred percent."

"Okay." He stripped off his grass green, short-sleeved polo and went straight to work.

I sat and pretended he wasn't half-naked, which was on the difficult side because he did have the six-pack I had suspected he would. Logan looked like a guy who worked out to keep fit, but not to excess. He had some good muscle definition going on.

He scrubbed my car down, rinsed, and began drying it. "How's Sunny?"

"She's good. Already back at work."

He nodded, squatting down to dry the passenger door. It was quiet until he'd finished drying everything. "Soames mentioned you're not seeing Nick anymore."

Logan tilted his head, surveying the quarter panel, and bent to buff a spot.

"Yeah, we broke up. Kind of got tired of the arguing, and his thinking I'm too dumb to survive much longer." Nearly the instant I said it, I realized how stupid that sounded, after my Near Death by Merriven experience. "Though I guess he has a point, huh?"

Logan glanced my way, not making eye contact or appearing to ogle my bikini-clad body. "I don't know about that. Talking the gargoyle into helping out was smart."

"I guess." Too bad I hadn't managed to completely impress upon Tase's mother, Petra, the need for quick action. She'd almost arrived too late.

He moved the microfiber towel a few inches to rub at another spot. I squinted, but couldn't see any leftover drops of water anywhere on my car, at least not the parts visible from where I sat. On the other hand, I had an excellent view of his muscles moving around under his tanned skin as he worked.

Hurray for car washing and a shirtless Logan. My day was definitely looking up.

"Heard anything about the house you wanted?"

"Hm?" I jerked my eyes away from his abs, hoping he hadn't noticed my ogling. He stepped back to scan the hood of my car. "Oh, yeah. Looks like it's a go. The owner's eager to sell, so Dad was able to talk him down a little more."

"Great. How long before you move in?"

"I don't know. Maybe another month or so. There's a lot of paperwork to it."

"We appreciate you putting us in contact with Rita. She's already been a huge help." Logan stretched over the hood to swipe the towel at a few spots. I tried to avoid staring and found myself doing it anyway, because of the way his jeans clung to his rear and thighs.

"Oh, good." My gosh, what was wrong with me? Too weak to finish washing my car, but not to drool all over a friend? Still needed to have that talk with myself about priorities and being shallow.

Said friend was pretty damn hot, and hotness wasn't remotely his best quality. Nope, there was compassion, his willingness to help others, strength, how he never freaked out about anything...a whole laundry list of great qualities, plus he liked to read.

"When you move, I'm available to do any heavy lifting you need done."

"Sure, if you'll do it shirtless too." My eyes widened. Holy crap. "Um, did I just say that out loud?"

"Yeah." Logan began furiously buffing a headlight. "I can go shirtless if you want me to."

"What I want right now is for the ground to open up and swallow me, because I can't believe I said that. And to you, of all people."

"I don't mind."

"It was rude and pretty wrong considering I haven't been broken up with Nick for even a month yet. You know, I kind of jumped into things with him and look how that turned out." Oh my God, Cordi, just shut up! "I mean, at least we've known each other for a while."

Logan wasn't buffing anymore. He'd straightened and turned to look at me, the towel dangling from his hand. Brow lightly furrowed, he said, "Yes, we have."

"But I'm in the rebound zone right now, so really, really shouldn't be noticing how hot you are." Holy crap, why couldn't I stop talking? "And you are. Very."

"Thanks."

There was me, being all shallow again. "Not that being hot is all you've got going. You're a good person, and," Shut up, shut up, ⬜⬜ ⬜! "You like to read too."

Logan held up his hand before I could blurt anything else out, and my teeth clicked as I forced my traitorous mouth shut. "I'm not sure what's going on right now."

Right. It wasn't as though all he'd said was he'd go shirtless if I wanted him to. That wasn't exactly an invitation to anything, and here I'd gone off, babbling like I thought he wanted...something. Heat suffused my face and I looked down. "Um, I'm still goofy from the blood loss and maybe a little delusional?"

"Oh, because I thought it sounded like you might be saying you find me attractive."

"The ground can open any time now," I muttered.

"If that was the case, then it'd be okay for me to mention the attraction's mutual, right?"

What did he just say? I peeked at his face. "It is?"

"Yes."

"Oh. Uh," I floundered for something to say, my mouth not cooperating. "Um, cool."

Logan softly chuckled. "Unless I'm really wrong, it also sounds like you don't want to date anyone for a while."

Had I said that? Wait, yeah, I'd mentioned something about "rebound zone" and wasn't even sure it applied to me, since I was the one who'd done the breaking up. Yet..."Yeah. Need a little time to clear my head and stuff. You know, need to move and settle in too."

He nodded. "Right. But just to be clear, in a month or two, if I asked you to dinner...."

"I'll say yes." Way to sound desperate, Cordi. "I mean, if you do feel like asking me to dinner sometime. In the future."

"Good. In the meantime, we'll see each other anyway, since we're friends and clan."

"Yes."

His smile caused my heart to skip a beat. "Okay. Sounds good."

"Yeah." My palms were sweating and I had no way to dry them. "It does. Hey, do you want something to drink? We have lemonade, tea, and beer."

"Thanks, but I should get back. Just wanted to drop by, see how you were doing." He flapped the towel at my car. "And this is done."

"Thank you. It looks great."

"No problem." He looked around. "Want me to put this stuff away?"

Oh, yes, so I can watch you some more. Fortunately, those words didn't make it past my lips. "I'll get it here in a few."

"All right." Logan tossed the towel into the pile with the others, collected his shirt off the grass, and took one step toward me before freezing. "Ah...Sure you don't need any help?"

"No, I'll be fine." To my disappointment, he half-turned toward his truck.

"Okay. I should get going. Bye."

"Bye." No cheeking and kiss for me.

I returned his wave as he drove off, and giggled like a maniac for a few minutes.

Logan liked me. Wanted to date me.

Nick had been right. The thought of my ex-boyfriend curdled my excitement. Why, I had no clue. I hadn't lied to him. Logan had played no part in my decision to break things off. And it wasn't as though I'd ever gone spelunking in Logan's mind to find out whether he liked me more than as a friend.

Did it matter what Nick would think? We weren't going to get back together, and he'd quit the agency. He wasn't a part of my life anymore. I couldn't live my life making decisions based on whether I'd be hurting Nick's feelings or not. "Oh, crap."

Nope, I needed to worry about what Danielle would do, because she certainly wasn't going to be happy if Logan and I started seeing each other.

For that matter, Logan was nearly thirty. What if he was ready to settle down, wanted kids, and stuff? "Double crap."

Levering myself out of my chair, I began picking up the car washing things. It appeared borrowing trouble was a habit of mine. One I needed to break.

After all, I was alive, had a new home, friends, a job I loved, and now, a date with Logan to look forward to.

Not too shabby.

About the Author

A sword-toting alien with a fetish for fur and four-legged creatures, she writes fiction and spends entirely too much time distracted by shiny things online, like Twitter.

She prefers Netflix because there aren't any commercials and she can ignore all the reality series. As a voracious reader, she enjoys both ebooks and physical books, though her ebook collection doesn't require regular dusting.

She writes scifi as G. L. Drummond, fantasy as Gayla Drummond, and other things as Louise Drummond.

If you're interested in news and future releases, you can find her on Facebook (http://www.facebook.com/G.L.Drummond), Twitter (@Scath), or visit her author web site at http://gldrummond.com.

The Discord Jones urban fantasy series has its own web site at http://discordjones.com.

www.ingramcontent.com/pod-product-compliance
Lightning Source LLC
Chambersburg PA
CBHW071253130626
46556CB00003B/1288